"You'd like to try all ten fantasies with me?" Callum asked with a grin

Josie's blush was beautifully telling. "Well, I...I..."

He waved the racy magazine at her from where he sprawled naked on the bed. "We've covered number one already, sweetheart. Last night. Sex With A Stranger. I was your stranger—though we're great friends now."

Josie laughed even as she recalled every delicious detail of the night. "I guess that's true."

"So that leaves nine more fantasies—one for every night I'm still in town." He paused. "Let's see, I'll pick you up at seven tonight. We'll go out for dinner."

"Out? Why don't we just stay here?" *In bed,* she thought.

"Oh, no. Fantasy number two is Sex In A Public Place. Wear a dress. Something soft and floaty. And no panties."

Callum loved seeing the mixture of shock and excitement in Josie's eyes. By the time seven o'clock came tonight, she'd be almost unbearably aroused.

And boy, so would he!

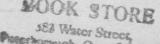

Dear Reader,

I once read a fascinating book that listed and explored all sorts of female sexual fantasies. They were many and varied, and I couldn't see some ever making the transition from fantasy to reality—physically Impossible! When I sat down to write my second Blaze book about a frustrated girl who had a sexual wish list a mile long, I wanted her fantasies to be the kind that could be fulfilled, if only she could find the right man.

Of course, I was eager to supply Josie with her Mr. Right. Not a fantasy man, either. But a real flesh-and-blood guy with the expertise and attitude for a no-strings, fantasy-fulfilling affair. Callum McCloud fitted the bill perfectly. Up to a point. He warns our heroine up front he isn't into Forever After. *No way. Never in a million years!* Yes, I can see you smiling. You know better, don't you? But the road to romance is a wild one, and Josie and Callum have many nights of wonderful sex before they embrace love. Wow, do they have fun together! Hope you have fun, too....

Miranda Lee

Books by Miranda Lee

HARLEQUIN BLAZE
9—JUST A LITTLE SEX...

HARLEQUIN PRESENTS
2212—FUGITIVE BRIDE
2236—A SECRET VENGEANCE
2242—THE SECRET LOVE-CHILD

A MAN FOR
THE NIGHT

Miranda Lee

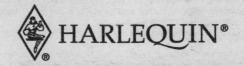

HARLEQUIN®

TORONTO • NEW YORK • LONDON
AMSTERDAM • PARIS • SYDNEY • HAMBURG
STOCKHOLM • ATHENS • TOKYO • MILAN • MADRID
PRAGUE • WARSAW • BUDAPEST • AUCKLAND

ISBN 0-373-79068-6

A MAN FOR THE NIGHT

Visit us at www.eHarlequin.com

Printed in U.S.A.

1

MEN WERE A LOST CAUSE, Josie Williams decided as she drove to work that Monday morning.

"At least where I'm concerned," she muttered.

She should have known Angus was too good to be true. Past experience should have warned her to look for the hidden flaws instead of hoping that she'd finally found her rainbow pot of gold—male-wise.

All that glitters had certainly not been gold on this occasion. Angus had been fool's gold, and she had been the fool. Again.

Josie sighed a weary sigh. At the rate she was going, she'd never find what she was looking for in a man. She was already twenty-eight, for pity's sake, with one failed marriage behind her, plus a string of so-so boyfriends.

"I'm jinxed," she grumbled as she turned her car into the suburban street where she had an appointment to meet Kay at nine-thirty.

A glance at the clock on the dash showed it was already nine-forty. She was running late, the result of an uncharacteristic case of Mondayitis. Usually, Josie couldn't wait to get up and go to work on a Monday, especially now that she was working for herself.

But when the alarm went off this morning, she'd

lain in bed for quite some time, thinking about the fiasco with Angus the previous night and trying to come to terms with the ongoing disaster of her personal life.

Was it her? Was she really jinxed? Or did she just want too much in a man?

Probably, Josie decided. Hadn't she always? But the truth was she simply couldn't bring herself to settle for less than what she'd always dreamt about, which was true love, plus her concept of a great sex life.

Not that she talked about this last part of her wish list anymore. Josie had come to the conclusion that her notion of a great sex life was outside the norm. So she kept the extent of her desires a deep dark secret. No way did she want her friends looking at her the same way her ex-husband had on their honeymoon, like she was some kind of raving nympho. When her girlfriends asked her what she wanted in a man, she now just said commitment and caring.

Even with this abbreviated wish list, Deb and Lisa said she was looking for something that didn't exist. Which might or might nor be true. Josie was loath to take her two late-twenties-and-still-single roommates' word for it.

Deb—a stylish blonde, but boyfriendless for over a year now—was the most cynical of the two. She thought all Australian men were selfish, and their idea of commitment and caring was remembering their current girlfriend's name while they were bedding her. Lisa, a curvy bottle redhead who'd only recently split with her latest boyfriend after finding him in bed with his next-door neighbor, was going through an I-hate-*all*-men phase.

Josie was infinitely grateful that she was house-sitting at the moment while her parents were away, which meant she wouldn't see Deb and Lisa till Wednesday, on their weekly girls' night out. She simply couldn't have coped with their toxic mixture of sympathy and sarcasm today. She could hear them now, spouting a fresh load of cutting comments about Aussie men and their shortcomings.

Thank goodness Kay didn't talk like that, Josie thought as she spotted her co-worker up ahead, waiting by her car. Kay Harper believed in Aussie men, plus their ability to truly love a woman. An understandable point of view, considering Kay was married to one fantastic man, Colin. Josie might have been jealous of her one and only employee if Kay hadn't been such a nice person.

Sliding her silver car into the blessedly empty spot behind Kay's navy two-door, Josie waved over at her through the windscreen. Kay waved back, a ready smile on her cutely pretty face.

Although thirty-five, Kay was often taken for much younger, courtesy of her elfin features, slight figure and short, layered blond hair.

Not that she'd been born a blonde, like Deb. Kay was a believer in the adage that what you didn't like about yourself, you changed. She'd also had a nose job in her twenties.

"Sorry I'm late," Josie said with an apologetic smile as she jumped out from behind the wheel.

"Slept in." Too late, Josie realized that was a leading thing to say.

Kay's blond tinted brows lifted in a suggestive fashion. "Really? That sounds promising. Do I take it you had a good night with Angus?"

Josie winced. What to say? Stupid to lie. But truly, she didn't want to have some lengthy postmortem over what had happened with Angus, even with Kay. Best she get this over and done with as swiftly and painlessly as possible. "Actually, no, I didn't."

"Oh? What happened?"

"We ran into a former lover of his."

"Oh dear. How awkward."

"You have no idea. The former lover was a man."

"*What?*" Kay looked almost as shocked as Josie had been at this discovery. "But…but I didn't know Angus is gay."

They'd both met Angus when Josie sought his services a couple of months back to revamp her company's Web site. And both had thought him a hunk of the first order.

Kay's shock quickly gave way to outrage. "If he is gay, then what the devil was he doing asking *you* out?"

"He claims he's not gay," Josie said dryly. "He's just bisexual. Likes both gals and guys, often at the same time, and was I interested in a little threesome?"

Kay grimaced. "Oh, yuck."

"My sentiments exactly." As wild as some of Josie's sexual fantasies were, they were always one-on-one with a heterosexual partner. Still, she had to wonder what it was about her that made Angus think she would be interested in that kind of thing. Perhaps it was the enthusiastic way she'd kissed him back on their last date. Whatever else he had been, Angus had been one very good kisser.

"I'll bet you're glad you kept to your no-sex-before-your-third-date rule," Kay said ruefully before flashing Josie an alarmed glance. "You *did* keep to that rule with him, didn't you?"

"Yes. Thank heavens. But last night was our third date and I was considering it. I shudder now just thinking about how close I came to an even greater disaster than my usual. I mean…I've picked some dud boyfriends in the past, especially in the bedroom department, but I've never picked a risk to my health!"

"A miss is as good as a mile."

Josie rolled her eyes. "I'm finding it difficult to play the glad game this morning, Miss Pollyanna."

"It's the only way, sweetie. After all, there's no real harm done, is there? It's not as though you were in love with the man."

"How do you know?"

"I remember what I was like when I first fell in love with Colin. You haven't been like that with Angus."

"Like what?"

"Distracted from your work. You'll know when you're truly in love, Josie, and so will I. Because your head will always be somewhere other than on the job. So far, in the time I've worked for you, that hasn't happened."

"No, I guess it hasn't," Josie conceded. "And I'm beginning to doubt if it ever will."

"It will. There are plenty more fish in the sea."

"That's what you always say. But I have a feeling all the really attractive guys in Sydney are gay."

"Rubbish! Sydney is chock full of good-looking straight guys."

"Yeah. But they're already married to clever women like you. And speaking of your being clever," Josie swept on, deciding a change of subject was called for, "you're going to have to be a very clever little decorator with this job I've lined up for us."

"Oh-oh. That sounds ominous."

"I have every confidence in you. After you've finished with this place, I'm sure it'll sell for well over the reserve. Come on. Let's go inside and I'll show you our new challenge firsthand." And she shepherded Kay into the square three-storey red brick apartment building which housed PPP's new project.

"What's the reserve price?" Kay asked with worry in her voice within a minute of stepping through the second floor apartment's front door.

Josie gnawed at her bottom lip. She had to confess that the place looked much worse today than when she'd inspected it on Saturday. Of course, at the time, she'd been in a state of pre-date excitement. On top of that the sun had been shining, making the most of the ocean view and brightening up the starkly empty rooms.

Today was overcast in more ways than one.

"Josie?" Kay prompted as she opened and closed one of the battered kitchen cupboards.

Josie shrugged off the gathering clouds of pessimism, determined not to fall victim to such self-destructive emotion. She'd been there, done that after her divorce, and she didn't want to go down that road again.

Admittedly, it was hard not to feel some dismay over her personal life this morning. She wouldn't be human if she didn't wonder and worry if she'd ever find someone even remotely close to her ideal man.

But no way was she going to let negative thinking creep into her working life. Work was the one thing she knew she could depend on. Work had always boosted her self-esteem and it gave her considerable satisfaction. Which was a lot more than any man had ever given her.

This project had been a good idea on Saturday, and it was still a good idea!

"Four hundred and ninety-five thousand," she said with renewed conviction.

Kay swung round with wide blue eyes. "You have to be kidding. For *this* dump?"

"It's not a dump in the real estate world," Josie pointed out firmly. "It's a two-bedroom apartment overlooking Manly Beach. A similar property sold at auction this last weekend for five hundred and seventy thousand."

"I'll bet it wasn't in this condition."

"No, of course not. Which is where we come in."

"But you said the auction's a week from Saturday. That hardly gives us much time. Less than two weeks…"

"It's more than enough time," Josie insisted. "And it's not as though we haven't done several similar jobs before. We have." *Property Presentation Perfect* specialized in this kind of makeover.

Which was what Josie had told the real estate agent on Saturday, backing up her claims with PPP's photographic portfolio of before and after shots. When he'd still looked doubtful, Josie had made him an offer any astute businessman could not refuse.

"If there's no sale at the upcoming auction, there's no fee. If the sale goes through, PPP gets a flat fee of five thousand dollars plus ten percent of the amount achieved over and above the reserve."

Josie wouldn't normally have offered such generous terms, but PPP was going through a bit of a slump during their second year of business. Which was one of the reasons she'd had their Web site revamped. Competition for the renovation dollar was very high in Sydney at the moment. With the proliferation of do-it-yourself shows on television, a lot of people now did their renovations themselves, rather than call in professionals.

Till business hopefully picked up again, Josie had started canvassing for work the old-fashioned way, calling on real estate agents face-to-face. She'd started with the major agencies on Sydney's lucrative North Shore, on the assumption that each was sure to have a wealthy client or two off-loading run-down rentals which could do with a facelift. So far, however, she'd only found this one Realtor willing to give PPP a try. But he'd said if the idea worked out, he would be happy to recommend her to other clients and industry contacts.

"We need to make a success of this," Josie told

Kay. "Otherwise, you might have to find a job elsewhere and I'll have to go back to working for Dad."

Kay gasped. "Lord. The pressure! Well, it'll certainly be a challenge," she added wryly. "This décor is ancient. The tiles in the bathroom are pink and gray, for pity's sake. As for this kitchen…" She waved a disparaging hand around the dingy and outdated layout. "It's fit for the scrap heap."

"Not after you've waved your magic wand," Josie encouraged. The things Kay could achieve with a paintbrush were limitless. "With the right color scheme and furniture, this place will look like a million dollars."

Kay laughed. "Who's the optimist now?"

Josie shrugged. "No point in being otherwise. You said as much yourself. So stop being so negative!"

"Aye aye, Captain Courageous. But just remember, we have less than two weeks to achieve this miracle, meaning we have no chance of hiring our usual tradesmen. They're booked up weeks in advance."

"No worries," Josie countered blithely. "We can't afford too many tradesmen on this occasion, anyway. We'll have to do most of the work ourselves. Our budget will just stretch to an electrician and a plumber, and the agent said we could use his. They're on permanent standby to repair all his agency's rentals. Otherwise, it's just you and me, baby," Josie said, linking arms with Kay and grinning down into her co-worker's pained face.

Kay looked up at her much taller boss and laughed. "Like I said, you certainly weren't in love with Angus. But speaking of that devil, what have you decided to do about next Saturday night? I mean…you haven't got anyone to take to your class reunion now, have you?''

THE INSTANT and very intense dismay which claimed Josie's face made Kay realize her boss had forgotten all about her class reunion. Which showed that underneath her boss's let's-get-on-with-life facade this morning, she was really quite upset.

Kay's heart went out to her. She knew how much Josie had been looking forward to taking Angus to her ten-year class reunion. And she knew the reason why.

The last—and only other time—Josie had gone to a class reunion had been five years back, shortly after her marriage had broken up.

She'd confided to Kay how awful she'd looked— and felt—that night; like a total failure in the face of her other classmates' seeming successes, especially this one girl, Amber, who'd made a grand entrance at the party on the arm of her communication tycoon fiancé.

Apparently, this Amber had been Josie's nemesis at school, a snooty-nosed golden-haired rich bitch who never let a chance go by to make Josie feel like an inferior species. Given that Amber was hosting this year's bash at her harborside mansion—she was now married to said tycoon—Kay could well understand Josie's distress.

''I don't suppose you could go alone again, could you?'' she said without much hope of that happening. Yet really, Josie shouldn't think she was a failure without a man on her arm. She ran her own business, for heaven's sake.

Josie's face showed horror at the suggestion. "I'd rather be thrown to the lions, because that's exactly what it would be like. Being thrown to the lions. Or the lioness, to be precise."

"You mean because of Amber, I suppose, the esteemed hostess of this masochistic do. You know, I used to work with someone like her. She hated my guts, mostly because I was a better interior decorator than she was. I dare say the same thing applies here, Josie. Your society princess felt threatened by you at school. You made *her* feel inferior, not the other way around. She saw you as competition."

"Who, me? I can't see how. Trust me when I say Amber Sinclair didn't have any competition at school. Besides being the best-looking and most popular girl in our class, she was smart. The girl has brains, Kay. She's not just some blond bimbo. The only thing I ever beat her at was math. But she beat me in every other subject. I can't understand why I got up her nose so much. I really can't."

"Try looking in the mirror sometime, then."

"But I wasn't at all good-looking at school, Kay. Honest. I was gawky back then. Too tall and too thin, with a flat chest and far too big a mouth." In every way, Josie recalled ruefully.

She'd had a tendency to speak her mind more than the average teenager, a consequence of being the only child of intelligent and loving parents. She'd joined in adult conversations since she was quite young and had been encouraged to have opinions.

Having opinions, however, guaranteed to make you an outsider at the rather old-fashioned all-girls' school to which she'd won a scholarship. You got along much better if you were a docile little sheep, or the beautiful and brilliant daughter of a billionaire banker who'd donated a million dollars for the new science wing.

"Well, you've certainly grown into your looks now, girl," Kay said, looking her boss up and down. "*And* your figure." Josie was that rare creature, a natural beauty who would look good first thing in the morning or straight out of the shower, without any artificial adornment. Her long straight black hair needed no blow-drying to look fabulous. Her olive skin could easily go without makeup, as could her long-lashed, slanting, near-black eyes. And her mouth, which she claimed was too big, would be the envy of every model. Full lips were the in thing these days.

All in all, Josie presented an exotic and very striking package without having to make too much personal effort. She didn't even exercise to keep her tall, just-curvy-enough body in shape.

Kay, on the other hand, had to work very hard to achieve her petite, fair-haired prettiness.

"My looks are not the issue here," Josie pointed out wearily. "It's my going alone."

An idea came to Kay. "Then don't go alone."

Josie eyed her warily. "Why are you smiling at me like that? What are you thinking of, you wicked woman?"

"Something deliciously devious."

"You're going to lend me Colin for the night?"

"Do I look insane? Not on your life, girl! It took

me thirty years to find my Prince Charming and he's not for hire. But hiring is the name of the game. You're going to hire yourself a drop-dead gorgeous male escort!''

''What? You're not serious.''

''I am indeed. I can even tell you which escort agency to contact and who to ask for.''

''How on earth would you know that kind of information? You're a happily married woman!''

''Yes, but I have a cousin who isn't, and she's the one who gave me the lowdown recently on *Gentlemen Partners.*''

''*Gentlemen Partners!* Don't you mean *Gigolo Creeps?*''

''That's what I thought when I first heard about this place. But Cora assured me it's a very reputable agency with only genuine gentlemen on their books. Most of the escorts are aspiring actors or male models, trying to earn an extra dollar on the side till they make it in their field. Which is why they're so good-looking. Cora's used their services more than once.''

Josie laughed. ''I'll bet she has.''

''No, no, you've got the wrong idea. Sex is definitely not one of the services provided. Apparently, if there's even a whiff of scandal, that particular escort— and client—is off their books in a flash.''

''Your cousin still must be a very confident woman to hire various men, even as just escorts.''

''She's a rally-car driver, so she's no shrinking violet. She's also divorced, pushing forty and without a new man in her life as yet. She hates going to functions on her own, so occasionally she hires someone to go with her. Last weekend, she had to go to an industry awards dinner where she knew she'd run into her rally driver ex, so she hired this gorgeous young hunk—she said he was only in his midtwenties—and passed him off as her boy-toy lover. He's one of the aspiring young actors' brigade and had no trouble assuming the role. Cora said he enjoyed it. She also said her ex was as jealous as sin and she had the loveliest time."

Kay was pleased to see that Josie was beginning to be intrigued by the idea. "Clearly this guy would have no trouble pretending to be *your* boyfriend," she went on. "His name is Beau Grainger and Cora said he's so good-looking, it's almost criminal."

"I don't know, Kay. It doesn't seem right."

"What's wrong about it?"

"I'm not sure...."

"It's the perfect solution to your problem. You go to your class reunion and feel good at the same time."

"But it's not a *real* feel-good feeling. It's only pretend."

"So what's the alternative? Staying at home and feeling sorry for yourself and knowing that have-it-all Amber is out there thinking you didn't have the guts to face her? She wins. Again. Especially if she calls you later to find out why you didn't show up."

"She *would* do that, too."

"What pathetic excuse will you use? Not the truth, I'll bet. You'll lie. You'll pretend. Better to pretend my way than your way. Give your pride a break."

Josie gnawed at her bottom lip as she often did when she was thinking, or worrying. Kay wondered if

Josie realized that by the time she stopped, her bottom lip always looked fuller and sexier than ever.

Undoubtedly not. From what Kay could gather, Josie was unaware of the extent of her sex appeal. She never dressed sexily, or used her looks to her advantage. Not in the two years Kay had known her, anyway.

Frankly, the girl seemed to be a bit uptight about sex. She rarely brought the subject up herself, and she had these hard-and-fast rules about her sexual behavior, such as her no-sex-till-the-third-date rule.

That was fine as a rule, and possibly sensible in this day and age. But it did smack of a lack of spontaneity in that area. Kay could never imagine Josie coming on to a guy on a first date, for instance. Not like *she* had with Colin. Still, she and Colin had fallen in love with each other at first sight. Maybe, if Josie ever fell in love like that, she'd be a different woman.

Still, till then, she needed to loosen up a bit.

Daring to hire a guy as her boyfriend for the night, even on a pretend basis, might be a good start.

Josie kept looking doubtful, however. And finding excuses. "If this Beau Grainger is so good-looking, he'd already be booked up for this Saturday night."

"Maybe, but there are still plenty of other gorgeous guys on their books. Cora said she was able to go through their photo files on their computer data base and pick whatever one she liked the look of. Sounds kinda kinky, doesn't it?" Kay added with a cheeky grin. "Pity their services don't extend to sex, in a way."

Kay realized immediately that was rather an unwise

remark. It seemed Josie's sense of humor did not extend to the subject of sex.

Some assertiveness was called for, if they were to get over this hurdle then get back to work.

"Go on," Kay urged. "Call information and find out the agency's number right now. Then call them and see if the gorgeous Mr. Grainger is free. If so, book him. If not, then arrange to go in and pick out another handsome hunk who is."

When Josie just stood there, looking blank, Kay took out her own cell phone. Truly, no wonder the girl hadn't found Mr. Right. She didn't have enough get-up-and-go in that department. Odd, really. She had plenty of get-up-and-go in every other way.

"I'll make the inquiries for you," Kay offered.

It didn't take her long to get through, or to find out that Beau Grainger had no bookings for the following Saturday night.

"He's free," she whispered to Josie. "What do you want to do?"

"Huh?" Josie blinked. She could hardly think. Kay's comments about choosing a guy off a computer had triggered a fantasy in her head unlike any she'd ever had before. In it, she'd hired a man whose looks she'd fancied, not as an escort, but as a lover. For one night. To do everything she'd always wanted a man to do to her.

For the first time in Josie's life, love didn't enter into her fantasy world. Neither did caring or commitment. Physical pleasure was the name of the game, with her partner a perfect stranger, a tall dark-haired stranger, with sexy blue eyes, a Bondi Beach tan and more bedroom know-how than Casanova. He was older than her, of course. Sex was his profession and his client's satisfaction was his first priority.

''Do you want to hire this Beau Grainger to take you to the reunion, or not?'' Kay demanded impatiently.

Josie dragged her mind out of the flames of her fantasy and back into cold hard reality, which was her class reunion next Saturday night, plus whether she should hire, not some gigolo to make love with her every which way, but a handsome hunk to salve her pride.

Not showing up was not a good option. When Brenda had called her just last week to check final numbers for the caterer—Brenda was this year's class reunion organizer and Amber's devoted dog-slave at school—Josie had stupidly boasted she'd be coming with her boyfriend.

The only positive thing about this awful situation was that she hadn't mentioned Angus's name. Josie supposed she *could* get away with showing up with any presentable male, as long as he was prepared to pretend he was her boyfriend. Which this Beau Grainger was obviously willing to do, since he'd been happy enough to pretend to be an older woman's boy-toy lover.

''Josie?'' Kay prompted.

Josie squared her shoulders. ''Here. Give me the phone,'' she said, and held out her hand.

Kay grinned and handed it to her. ''Go for it, girl!''

Josie rolled her eyes. It wasn't a question of going for anything. It was a question of pride.

2

CALLUM MCCLOUD HAD MIXED FEELINGS every time he flew into Sydney. Coming home was a two-edged sword, his pleasure at seeing his kid brother again always tempered by a niggling concern over what Clay might have been up to since his last visit.

Not that there'd been any nasty surprises on his last few visits. The problem was Callum couldn't forget what had been waiting for him the first couple of times he'd come home after taking on his present job three years back.

Frankly, he would never have accepted an overseas position if he'd imagined that as soon as his back was turned, his brother would leave university to try an acting career. At the time, Clay had already turned twenty-one and was well into his medical degree, seemingly happy and settled.

Callum had been aware that his younger brother had once harbored a secret ambition to be the next Australian male actor to take Hollywood by storm. But he'd thought the boy had grown out of that pie-in-the-sky dream.

Not so, apparently.

To give him some credit, Clay had stuck to his guns, insisting that being a doctor had been their mother's ambition, not his, and he shouldn't be held to a death-bed promise that Callum had made, not him.

"You're my *brother,* Cal," Clay had pointed out. "Not my father. Let me make my own mistakes in life. This is what I want to do, so butt out!"

Although believing Clay was making a major mistake, Callum had finally agreed to support his decision, though not to the extent of working his own butt off and paying for everything while Clay went around going for endless and probably futile auditions. Clay admitted he'd already tried for and been rejected by NIDA, which showed what the most highly regarded acting school in Australia thought of his acting ability.

"You can stay on in my house in Glebe, rent-free," Callum had grudgingly offered. "The house *my* hard work bought and renovated, might I add. But you'll have to find a part-time job to pay for your food and clothes."

Which Clay had.

Callum had gone back overseas that first time, believing Clay was flipping hamburgers in a local fast-food restaurant, only to come home a few months later to find him working as a male model for a famous swimwear company.

Callum wasn't a narrow-minded man, just a very male one. The thought of his brother walking up and down the catwalk in skin-tight briefs just didn't sit well on him.

And he'd said so.

"But the money's good, bro," Clay countered. "And I'm not about to turn gay, if that's what you're worrying about. Trust me on that."

Callum did trust him on that. He'd been finding scantily-clad girls in his brother's bedroom since the boy hit puberty. That wasn't the point. The point was Clay had promised to stay put at the hamburger job, but as soon as Callum's back was turned, he was off doing something else, something which he obviously thought he had to keep secret from his brother. Why?

"I've read about the modeling world," Callum had commented at the time. "It's full of drugs."

"No more than the university," Clay shot back. "And I didn't do drugs there. Stop being so paranoid."

"I'm not being paranoid. I'm just doing what our mother asked me to do. Looking after you."

When Clay rolled his eyes at this and once again launched into his you're-my-brother-not-my-father speech, Callum stopped arguing with him. After all, Clay was technically right. He wasn't his father, though he'd felt like one ever since their real father had walked out on his family when Clay had been barely two months old. Callum—six, at the time—had suddenly found himself the man of the house, a role which he'd shouldered to the best of his ability. He'd been more father than brother to Clay for all of his life, a role which Clay obviously resented.

But someone had to keep an eye on the boy. Clay was far too good-looking for his own good. And not worldly-wise enough, in Callum's opinion. Survival in the modeling—and acting—world required a level head on your shoulders. And a degree of maturity Callum had yet to see in his kid brother.

So here he was, still keeping an eye on him. Clay

was no longer strutting his stuff as a male model, courtesy of a new agent who'd been getting him some real acting work, both on TV and in the movies. He'd been all good news over the phone the last few months. Not quite so chirpy yesterday, however, when Callum had phoned to let him know his estimated time of arrival.

Callum jerked his luggage trolley to a halt. Was that what had been niggling away at his subconscious during the flight home? Had his big-brother antenna instinctively tuned into some problem Clay had been trying to hide from him?

"You got a problem there, buddy?"

Callum took a second or two to realize that the customs officer was talking to him.

"Nope," he returned, and pushed his trolley up to the customs desk.

"At least I sure hope not," he muttered under his breath shortly after as he made his way down the walkway toward the arrivals terminal.

Clay was there, waiting for him, which was a surprise in itself, given it was seven o'clock on a Saturday morning. Early rising was not one of Clay's virtues. Neither was being on time for unimportant things such as picking up his brother at the airport.

When Clay smiled, waved, and rushed over to him, Callum's suspicion increased. This was a welcome fit for a pop star, or a big brother who needed sucking up to.

"Great to see you again, bro," Clay greeted, throwing his arms around him and giving him a big hug.

"Great to see you, too," Callum returned, drawing back to inspect his brother's face closely for signs of dissipation and drugs. Fortunately, that didn't seem to be the trouble. Clay was looking fit and healthy, his blue eyes as clear and bright as a cloudless summer sky.

Callum ran a few other possible problems through his mind. Clay had borrowed and crashed his big brother's prized car? Run up a colossal phone bill? Gotten one of his girlfriends pregnant?

Surely *that* wasn't the case. If there was one thing Callum had drummed into his kid brother it was the need for safe sex. Given the dubious circles he was now moving in, using protection was more important than ever. Callum had stressed this the last few times he'd been home.

"Man, but *you're* looking good," Clay complimented him with what Callum felt was decidedly false enthusiasm. Clay never gave a damn what he looked like. "Fantastic tan. Working in Hawaii agreed with you. Bet you're sorry you're all finished up there now."

"Nope," Callum said, more and more sure that something was up with his brother. "I'm always glad to move on."

Which was true.

Callum loved his work as a traveling trouble-shooter for INCON, an American company which specialized in building shopping malls all over the world. He thrived on the challenges the job presented, finding great satisfaction in solving whatever engineering problems needed to be solved. But he also liked the constant changes in his lifestyle, the living in different places and meeting different people.

Most guys his age—he would turn thirty-one next birthday—started looking to settle down in one place, get married, have a family.

But that was not for him. Not ever.

"So where to next time?" Clay asked, keeping up his uncharacteristic chitchat about Callum's life. Usually, the only person he talked about was himself. "What fabulous part of the world are they sending you off to next?"

"Don't know yet. I have to go back to head office in San Francisco first."

"When will that be?"

Callum wondered why that mattered. "A week from Tuesday," he said. "Don't worry, if you have to work that day, I can always catch a taxi to the airport."

"No, no. No sweat. Tuesdays are always fine." He flashed Callum one of his winning smiles. "So what are you going to do for the next ten days? Paint Sydney red?"

Callum knew his brother was mocking him. Clay thought he was a stick-in-the-mud, but Clay didn't know him at all. Not the real him. He only knew the persona Callum adopted in his role as big-brother-cum-father-figure. He was a different person when he was away, when he wasn't burdened by the feeling he had to set a good example for his brother, especially where the opposite sex was concerned. Clay would be very surprised if he knew the real facts of his brother's private life.

"Not this time," he replied dryly. "Between catching up on sleep and doing some surfing, I thought I might look around and buy myself another investment property. Got a pretty nice bonus last week.''

''No kidding. If you don't watch out, you'll own half of Sydney soon. Who would have imagined that being an engineer would pay so well? Still, being a Hollywood icon pays better,'' Clay added with a grin. ''When I'm making fifty mill a movie, I'll buy myself one of those fancy harborside mansions. You know, the ones with the pool, the tennis court and their own private yacht mooring.''

''Speaking of your becoming a Hollywood icon,'' Callum said as he swung his luggage trolley around and started heading for the exit. ''Are things still going reasonably well in the acting department? I didn't have time to ask you yesterday.''

''Yes and no. The character I was playing in that soap got canned and directors keep telling me at movie auditions that I'm *too* good-looking. But things could be about to look up.''

''In what way?''

''I'm going to this party tonight being thrown in honor of some visiting big boys from Hollywood. They're out here, searching for a young Aussie hunk to play the lead in their new blockbuster movie. Harry said I was just the type they were looking for and wangled an invitation so that they can see me in person. This particular director and producer have a reputation for 'finding' their stars in unconventional ways, not at formal auditions.''

''In that case, you won't be the only handsome young Aussie actor who just happens to be there tonight, Clay. I hope you realize that.''

"For crying out loud, do you ever get off being negative about my career? Look, I know the competition is tough, especially in Hollywood. I know the odds are stacked against me. But I still have to go for it. It's what I've always wanted to do, bro. *Always*. I know you think I'm just a pretty face but I'm a damned good actor too. Harry says I have what it takes, and Harry should know. He's represented the best."

"Okay, okay, don't get touchy. And I'm not being negative. I'm just being..."

"Bloody overprotective, as usual. Like I've always said, you're my brother, Cal, not my..."

"*Father,*" Callum finished for him ruefully. "Yes, yes, I know. So tell me some more about these Hollywood big boys. Who are they and what have they done and no, I'm not being nosy, just showing an interest."

In the five minutes it took to make their way from the terminal to where Callum's thankfully uncrashed car was parked, Clay never shut up long enough to draw breath. For the first time, Callum witnessed his brother's true passion for the film industry. He knew every movie this producer and director had collaborated on in minute detail, along with their personal backgrounds and future goals.

Callum began to finally understand that nothing was going to dissuade Clay from pursuing his dream, certainly not any of *his* warnings.

"You're really looking forward to going to this party tonight, aren't you?"

"You could say that," Clay replied. "If anything happened to stop me going, I don't know what I'd do."

Callum realized then what was bothering his brother.

It was just tension over this party.

"What could possibly stop you from going?" he asked as he loaded his three large suitcases into the trunk of his car. With the job finished in Hawaii, he'd had to bring everything home with him.

CLAY LOOKED OVER at his big brother and knew he was going to have a fit when he told him about his problem. Callum's reaction to his doing some male modeling had been bad enough. He was going to hit the roof when he found out his precious little brother had been working as an escort!

But he had to tell him; had to ask him to take his place, just for tonight. There was no other way. If he called the agency and canceled at this late stage his name would be mud. He also needed the money. He'd run up quite a bill on his credit card this last month, buying new clothes, first a tux for his escorting work, and then some seriously cool gear for this party tonight.

On top of that, as wimpish as it sounded, he didn't want to disappoint his client. She'd sounded really nice when he'd called her on Thursday night to find out what was required of him.

Unfortunately, his client's requirements presented an added problem, other than the obvious. Clay knew *he'd* have had no trouble pretending to be this girl's boyfriend at her class reunion. He viewed each of his escorting dates as opportunities to hone his acting skills. Callum, however, would balk at such a ruse. He was hard pushed to pretend anything in life. He was a straight shooter, was Callum, and as stuffy as could be. Clay wondered sometimes if his big brother even had a sex life, though he supposed he did. Callum was one hell of a good-looking guy in that tall rugged mould. Lots of women would be attracted to his good looks, and his impressively fit body. It was just that he rarely dated when he came home, and never talked about women and sex the way other guys did.

Getting him to go on a date as a paid escort and a pretend boyfriend at the same time was not going to be easy. On the plus side, Clay knew that his brother loved him and would do anything for him, within reason. He just had to make it all sound both respectable and reasonable.

"The problem is I have to work tonight."

Callum slammed the trunk shut, then glanced up, his dark brows drawn together over his deeply set blue eyes. "I thought you said you didn't have any acting work at the moment."

"I don't."

Callum groaned. "Oh, no, not more modeling work."

"No. Nothing like that."

"Then *what?*"

Clay crossed his fingers behind his back. "I've been working as a professional escort, and I have a pre-booked, pre-paid date tonight. I...er...was hoping you could take my place so that I could still go to the party."

Clay almost laughed at the look on his brother's face. Boy, was it a classic! He immediately slotted it into his acting memory bank for future reference, so that when a director told him to express shock, disgust, disbelief and indignant outrage all at the same time, he'd know exactly how to do it.

"Before you blow a fuse, bro," Clay went on hastily when he saw his brother's hands curl into fists, "let me point out that there are several groups of people close by in this carpark. I'll hardly make a good impression on my Hollywood big boys if I turn up tonight with a split lip and a black eye."

"I wasn't going to hit you," Callum bit out. "Though you need hitting, you stupid fool. My God, whatever possessed you? Silly question," he muttered under his breath. "I suppose it was for the money. But surely you couldn't have needed money that badly that you'd virtually prostitute yourself for it."

"Hey, get off your high horse there. Being an escort is *not* synonymous with being a prostitute. I work for a very reputable agency called *Gentlemen Partners,* and sex is definitely not part of the service provided."

"That's not the general view."

"Then the general view is wrong," Clay refuted firmly, though his mind did fly to that one date a couple of weeks back. He'd not only ended up in bed with the woman but the next morning she'd pressed an embarrassing amount of money into his hands, all because of some stupid joke he'd made when he'd brought her home the night before. He hadn't known what to do at the time. In the end, he'd just taken it and left.

Naturally, he wasn't about to mention that one unfortunate incident to Callum.

His brother still looked furious. "Tell that to the gossip mags if you ever get your name up in bright lights and they find out what you once did for a living!"

"You think I haven't thought of that? Why do you think I use a false name?"

Callum could not believe his brother's naiveté. What was a name when he had a face like his? So strikingly handsome and so very memorable. Maybe this escort agency he worked for was extremely respectable, but a lot of those places weren't. And mud did stick.

"How long have you been doing this?" Callum demanded to know. "How many of these...*dates*...have you been on?"

"Only half a dozen or so. I don't know what you're getting so het up about. It's an ideal job. I can earn money at night and still have my days free to call on casting agencies and go for auditions."

"Only ideal if you never make it big in Hollywood," Callum pointed out. "You keep telling me you are going to make it big in Hollywood, aren't you?"

"Too right I am."

"Then I'll make a deal with you. I'll stand in for you tonight if you quit the agency tomorrow and find some other line of work. Something which won't ever find its way into a gossip column. Fair enough?"

"Fair enough," Clay agreed, and beamed at his brother. "Thanks, bro. You're the best!"

Callum smiled a wry smile. Clay was always particularly agreeable after he got his own way. Or when Callum rescued him from whatever trouble he'd got himself into. In the past, Callum had stood up for his kid brother more times than he'd had hot dinners, but this was the first time he'd stood *in* for him.

One day, Callum hoped and prayed, he'd stop being his brother's keeper. But not yet, obviously.

"Keys," he said, holding out his hand.

"Ah, come on, bro, let me drive it home. I won't speed. I promise."

"No way, Jose. On the way home, you can tell me all about this stupid date I'm going on tonight. Where, what, when and who with? Which reminds me, what name is it you use for your escorting work? I suppose I'll have to use it too."

"Beau Grainger," his brother said, grinning.

Callum winced. The things he had to do!

3

JOSIE LAY BACK in the bubble-filled bathtub, trying to relax and not think about the night ahead. Because there was no going back now. The deed had been done. She'd already hired the guy. Paid for him, too, with her credit card.

Not that she really wanted to back out of the idea. Kay had been right. It was the only way that she could go to the reunion and save her pride.

But it was a bold thing to do. And kind of scary. Beau Grainger might be a good actor and very adept at pretending to be a boyfriend. He'd obviously done a good job as a boy-toy lover. But could *she* successfully pretend to be *his* girlfriend?

She'd only spoken to him briefly the other night and while he'd seemed quite nice, she didn't know anything about him except that he was twenty-four, and an out-of-work actor. They would have to exchange quite a few more details about each other and each others' families on the drive from here to Elizabeth Bay, then invent a more suitably successful career for him, because Amber was sure to give her and her "boyfriend" the third degree.

Josie began to worry about that third degree. What if they slipped up and Amber twigged that their relationship was a charade? Even worse, what if someone there recognized Beau from another of his escorting jobs? When she thought about it, the idea was fraught with flaws and possible failings. Whatever had possessed her to agree to Kay's urgings?

Was it too late to cancel?

People probably canceled at the last minute all the time. But Kay was going to call her in the morning to see how things went. Having to tell her she'd pulled out was not on.

No, it was all systems go and there was no point in worrying about it anymore. In less than three hours, she'd be arriving at her class reunion on Beau Grainger's arm, and that was that.

Feeling better for her self-lecture, Josie leaned forward through the vanilla-scented bubbles and reached for the magazine resting on the side of the tub. It was one of those glossy women's magazines which featured sex on every second page, alongside pictures of skinny models in unflattering poses.

Lisa had given this one to her last Wednesday night. Both Josie's roommates were addicted to the things, especially the advice columns, which had letters from girls with even more pathetic relationships than they had. They claimed reading about other females' miseries and mistakes made them feel better. However, Josie could really identify with that this week and was flipping over the pages to find the advice column first when her eyes were caught by the sealed section in the middle—that had been torn open!

STARTLING RESULTS OF OUR RECENT SEX

SURVEY, the banner headline screamed. Then underneath, SEE WHAT IT IS WOMEN *REALLY* WANT!

Josie recalled Lisa mentioning that particular article when she'd handed over the magazine. Of course, men and sex were Lisa and Deb's staple subjects of conversation, especially over drinks.

"Talk about hot stuff!" Lisa had exclaimed after downing her third cocktail. "But it makes you think. I mean...there are women out there actually getting that kind of thing. Amazing! I wish I could find a guy who'd deliver half of what's listed in that survey."

"Half!" Deb had crowed. "I'd settle for a quarter!"

Josie's curiosity had been aroused at the time and she'd meant to read the article when she got home that night. But she'd just been too tired. She and Kay had been working extra hard all week, preparing then painting the walls of the apartment. By the time she'd arrived home after spending a couple of hours in a bar with her friends, she'd just collapsed into bed. Not even reading about unbelievably hot sex would have kept her awake.

But what better subject to get her mind off worrying about tonight? Josie had always enjoyed reading about sex. As a teenager, she'd devoured every sexy book she could find, living in avid anticipation of experiencing the joy of sex for real. Since reality hadn't delivered any actual joy so far, Josie figured she could at least have some vicarious pleasure via the pen, as opposed to the sword, so to speak!

Smiling wryly at her clever pun, Josie lifted her elbows onto the sides of the tub, leaned her head carefully back onto the folded towel she'd placed there earlier, and started to read.

The whole article, she quickly realized, was devoted to a series of top ten lists. They started off pretty tamely, the first list being the top ten sexiest guys in the world, followed by the top ten sexiest guys in Australia. All quite predictable, filled with well-known movie stars, singers and sportsmen.

None set Josie's heart a-thudding. She had her own idea of what the sexiest guy in the world would be like for her and it had nothing to do with those high-profile men. Her dream man was far more accessible. Far more real. He didn't have to be drop-dead handsome, just reasonably attractive, with a well-built body, a well-stoked libido and a fertile imagination.

Oh, and he had to be all hers. Had she mentioned that?

Like Deb and Lisa said, he probably didn't exist.

But she could dream, couldn't she?

Flicking the page over, Josie's darkly winged brows shot up when she saw the topic of the next list. Now *this* was more like it.

THE TEN SEXUAL POSITIONS MOST POPULAR WITH WOMEN.

AND WHY…

Josie worked her way through the list, her eyes widening as she read the variations and comments attached to each position.

"Oh my," she breathed huskily at one stage, "I didn't know that."

And how would you, girl? Your range of sexual

positions in your life so far stands at one. Man-on-top, woman-on-bottom. End of story!

Of course, she'd long *known* about all these other positions. Well…all except number five, that is. She'd never read about *that* one before.

It did irritate her, however, that the good old missionary position still made the list, and was raved over by several women. Raving certainly hadn't been the case in her experience. Still, maybe if she ever found some man who could do it well, she might change her mind. She'd sure like the opportunity to try one of the variations mentioned, the one with the woman's feet hooked over the man's shoulders.

Finds my G-spot every time, was the comment.

No man had ever found Josie's G-spot. She wasn't sure if she even had one. Still, not too many men had found her clitoris, either, and she was very sure she had one of those!

The next double-page spread held an even more eye-popping and envy-making list.

THE TEN THINGS WOMEN MOST LIKE MEN TO DO TO THEM IN BED!

Josie groaned. Talk about practicing masochism. If there were men out there who did such things to and for their women, then fate had been very unfair to her.

Josie's sexual partners so far had consisted of two wham-bang-thank-you-ma'am college students, one seriously undersexed and sanctimonious husband, plus a handful of poorly-informed and poorly-equipped boyfriends who didn't last enough dates to be called true boyfriends.

What she wouldn't give for one night with one of

the lovers discussed in *this* list, the kind of man who could blow a woman's mind, whatever that felt like. It was one of the remarks next to the number one thing women liked men to do to them in bed.

Josie could only dream about that activity as well. She'd never had the experience at all. Not once. Which was downright criminal, considering its ranking.

At this point, Josie wasn't sure if she wanted to read the rest of the article. She hated feeling jealous of other women.

On the positive side, at least she now knew that she wasn't abnormal. What she'd always wanted in bed was what a lot of other women wanted. And what far too many of the lucky ones got!

But who knew? Maybe some day, somewhere, she'd have some luck of her own and meet a man who would finally fulfil her sexual wish list.

Oh-oh, she was playing the glad game again! Kay would be proud of her. With a self-mocking laugh, Josie turned the page and confronted the last and longest list.

THE TOP TEN FEMALE SEXUAL FANTASIES!

Josie closed her eyes briefly, then opened them again. Might as well read the darned thing.

Actually, another small measure of relief came over Josie as she read the kind of sexual fantasies other women had. Not so very different from her own. Some were even wilder. Heck no, *most* of them were wilder. A couple were quite shockingly outrageous.

Of course, they were only fantasies. And fantasies weren't meant to be enacted for real. They were just fun for the mind. Vicarious pleasure. Imaginative thrills.

Josie's imagination immediately obliged and she was off in a highly erotic world when the phone rang.

Her first irritated thought carried regret that she hadn't thought to bring the mobile phone with her into the bathroom. Josie's second impulse was to ignore the ringing. But what was the point? The mood of the moment had been broken. Besides, it might be important. Her parents, maybe, calling her from wherever in the world they were at the moment.

Putting the magazine down, she climbed out of the bathtub, wrapped a towel around her bubble-covered body and hurried along to the master bedroom, and the nearest phone extension.

"Hi there," she answered, sweeping up the handset.

"Josie, it's Lisa. I know you're probably busy getting ready for tonight, but Deb and I just wanted to find out what you ended up buying to wear. Did you go and look at those two dresses I told you about?"

Lisa had told her last Wednesday night about two party dresses she'd seen in a boutique window near where she worked in the city, insisting that both would look fabulous on Josie. One was red and one was black, and she'd been right. They had both looked great. They were also a lot sexier than the sort of dress Josie usually wore.

Still, the knowledge that Amber would no doubt show up tonight wearing some fabulously expensive designer gown had prompted Josie to throw caution to the winds.

"You'll be pleased to know that I tried on both

dresses," Josie told her roommate, "and I bought one."

Lisa squealed with delight. "Fantastic! Which one? The slinky red or the sexy black?"

"The slinky red." And slinky it was, with its halter neckline and low, low back, making bra-wearing not an option. The black dress had been equally daring, being strapless and skin-tight, but it had been short. The invitation for the reunion had said black tie, which meant formal gowns—and formal generally meant long.

"Atta girl!" Lisa exclaimed. "I was worried you might buy something conservative. Wow, wait till Angus sees you in that tonight. He's going to flip."

Josie flinched. She'd lied by omission last Wednesday night, not telling Lisa and Deb a word about dumping Angus. And she certainly hadn't told them about hiring an escort to take her tonight instead. They'd never let her hear the end of it. She'd let them think she was still going with Angus.

Silly her. Now she'd have to come up with a real lie tomorrow—the three of them were meeting for Sunday brunch in the city. Maybe she could say that Angus admitted to being bisexual when he brought her home after the reunion and that she wouldn't be dating him anymore.

Yes, that would have to do.

Meanwhile, she didn't want to discuss the man. Or the reunion tonight. She was getting nervous again, now that her mind had been dragged back out of her perfect fantasy world and into imperfect reality.

"Are you going to sleep with Angus this time, do you think?" Lisa rattled on.

Josie pulled a face. Deception had a way of escalating, despite one's best efforts to contain it! "I...er... think I'll just wait and see how I feel."

"Gosh, I wish I had your control. But you don't like sex much, do you?"

Josie shouldn't have been surprised by this remark. If her roommates thought she was a bit of a cold fish where sex was concerned, then she had only herself to blame. But when she'd first met Deb and Lisa, she hadn't been long divorced from Peter, and was still suffering all sorts of mental torment from his constant accusations about her desires. It seemed better to give her new friends the impression she was a tad on the stuffy side, rather than have them think she was a sex maniac. Still, Josie now knew she wasn't a sex maniac at all, just a normal redblooded Aussie girl. Maybe it was time she redressed their misconception about her in that area.

"That depends," she said.

"On what?"

"On who I'm having sex with. With the right man, I'm sure I'd like sex a lot. It's just that I've been involved with some colossal duds when it comes to lovemaking so far."

"Yeah. I know what you mean. Most men don't measure up to our expectations. Still, maybe you'll get lucky tonight," Lisa went on eagerly. "You have one hot date there."

Josie wondered what had happened to Lisa's man-hating mood, but decided not to ask. Neither of her roommates ever really went off men for too long. They talked tough and bitter for a while after a breakup, but a good-looking guy only had to look their way and they fell in love all over again.

"I have to go, Lisa. I've just run a bath and it's getting cold. I'll see you tomorrow, okay?"

"Okay. Have fun now."

Fun! Fun was the last thing Josie anticipated having tonight. She'd be happy just getting through the evening without having everything blow up in her face.

4

CALLUM GAVE A LOW WHISTLE as he pulled his red car up outside the Castlecrag address his brother had given him. Ms. Josie Williams must have well-to-do parents to live here, he decided as he switched off the engine and glanced down the sloping front lawn to the large split-level home with its view of Middle Harbour.

Surely she couldn't own this home herself. Not at the age of twenty-seven or twenty-eight.

Callum had deduced Ms. Williams's age from the fact that tonight's event was her ten-year class reunion. It was a case of basic math, given most graduates of Australian high schools were seventeen or eighteen. He knew no other details about her except she wanted a fake boyfriend on her arm to take with her to said reunion.

Callum tapped his fingers on the steering wheel and speculated once again over the reasons why a girl would want to hire a fake boyfriend.

The one and only logical reason hardly made him look forward to this evening. She was obviously desperate and dateless, a poor little rich bitch with more money than looks or personality. In other words, a plain Jane and a bore, who had difficulty getting a date, let alone a boyfriend, but who was determined not to go to her class reunion all alone.

Which was where he came in.

When he'd expressed concern to Clay earlier this afternoon over being able to pull this charade off, his brother's advice was that he should simply treat the girl like a normal date.

"You do date occasionally, don't you, bro?" Clay had almost taunted.

Callum had growled that of course he did.

"I was beginning to wonder. There you go, then. Just do what you do on one of your regular dates."

Nice idea in theory, but Callum suspected Ms. Josie Williams would be nothing like any girl he'd ever dated. Callum only asked out confident career women who knew what they wanted, then went out and got it for themselves. Girls with balls, for want of a better word. Invariably beautiful, brainy and bold, they liked male company—and sex—but had no desire to marry at this stage in their lives. If ever.

Callum had had relationships with a series of such women over the past few years, and he'd remained friends with almost all of them after he'd moved on. Only once had he chosen poorly, a New York divorcée who had seemed an assertive independent spirit on the surface, but who was secretly a shattered and needy soul, ripe and ready to create havoc in Callum's life when the relationship ended.

Having a firsthand experience with that kind of *Fatal Attraction* scenario had made Callum a once-bitten, twice shy kind of guy, partly because he never wanted to be subjected to that kind of personal harassment again. But mostly because he didn't want to be responsible for hurting another woman like he'd obviously hurt Meg. He always made it his business these days to find out lots about a female before he asked her out, as well as keeping his eyes wide open during their first date. If there was any hint of emotional vulnerability or instability, then it was a peck on the cheek at the end of the night, and a swift *adieu*.

Callum suspected Ms. Josie Williams would disqualify herself from being a regular date of his on every level.

No, thinking of her as a regular date wasn't going to work. He'd have to do what he really wasn't all that good at.

Act.

Oh, well. He could only do his best. With a resigned sigh, Callum climbed out of his car, locked it and headed along the path which led past the garage and down some stone steps onto an L-shaped colonnaded porch.

The front door was in a recessed alcove, not visible from the street, with an elegant lamp light overhead, stained glass windows on either side and a doorbell in its middle. Callum pressed the button and waited. No one came, despite the rather loud chime echoing through the house.

Callum was about to press the bell again when the door was whisked open and he was confronted by a very different Josie Williams than the one he'd pictured. At least, he *assumed* the ravishing creature standing before him was Josie Williams, given she was around the right age and dressed to kill in a smashing red evening gown.

Wow! he thought, as his surprised eyes took in every inch of his date from the top of her shiny dark head to the tip of her open-toed high heels. This was one great-looking girl. She had it all. Long glossy black hair. Gorgeous olive skin. Sexy cat's eyes. Cute little turned-up nose. And a mouth to drive a man wild!

And that was just her face and hair.

Her figure was equally sensational, and exactly the way Callum liked a woman's body. Tall and slender, with narrow hips and breasts that were full without being top-heavy. His gaze returned to linger on those very nice and obviously braless breasts, which were cupped sexily by the cut of the dress, the halterneck style lifting them up and together into a very eye-catching cleavage.

Callum was certainly having trouble taking *his* eyes off her cleavage. Why such a hot-looking babe didn't have a real boyfriend to take her wherever she might want to go on a Saturday night was more than a mystery. It was a crime!

Whatever the reason, Callum's feelings toward the evening took a definite turn for the better. Of course, his date could be a total no-no in the brains department, but spending a few hours with her sure wouldn't be hard on his eyes. Or his ego.

"Ms. Williams, I presume," he said with a smile.

She smiled back—if a little nervously.

"Yes. That's right. And you must be Beau Grainger? Come in for a minute."

Callum nodded and followed her inside, privately

thinking it was going to be difficult answering to such a stupid name all evening.

"You're different from what I pictured," she said, a slight frown gathering on her high forehead as she looked him up and down.

He could have said the same about her.

"In what way?" he asked, wondering all of a sudden if she was disappointed. Maybe the agency had described Clay to her and she'd been expecting a real pretty boy. Or maybe she'd just formed a mental picture in her head from talking to his sweet-talking brother the other night on the phone. It was as well that their voices were similar or she'd be saying he sounded different as well.

"You look older," she told him.

"I've always looked old for my age," he said by way of an excuse. Naturally, he *did* look older than Clay's twenty-four. He was thirty, going on thirty-one.

"Does my looking older present a problem for you?" he added, the thought crossing Callum's mind that maybe she'd *wanted* a younger boyfriend on her arm. Who knew what her secret agenda might be? She certainly hadn't hired an escort because she couldn't get a date herself the normal way.

"Oh, no, no, not at all," she denied, but Callum thought he detected something in her expressive brown eyes. Guilt, perhaps? No, not guilt. Embarrassment. She was *embarrassed* by this situation.

Odd, since she was the one who'd orchestrated it.

"Better you do look older, I suppose," she went on a bit brusquely. "I mean, given that I'm twenty-eight and you're supposed to be my boyfriend."

Callum frowned over the puzzle of this stunning twenty-eight-year-old. "Would you mind my asking why a girl like yourself doesn't have a boyfriend for real?"

She laughed a small, dry laugh. "In actual fact, I *did* have a boyfriend. Till last weekend."

"What happened?"

Her eyes flashed with remembered anger. "I found out he didn't want what I wanted, and we came to an abrupt parting of the ways."

"Aah…" Callum didn't need to ask any more questions. Relationships were not easy, and many ended badly and prematurely, especially for the girls who wanted wedding bells and baby bootees. And, let's face it, a lot of them did.

Most guys weren't in any rush to get to the altar. Nowadays, the singles scene was a sexual smorgasbord and men tended to put off marriage till they themselves wanted to settle down and have a family. Most girls, however, were different.

At twenty-eight, Josie Williams was already at that age where she'd be seriously looking for a husband, whereas it was highly likely that all her boyfriend had had in mind was more fun and games.

"You didn't have any other male friend you could ask to take you to your reunion?" Callum continued, wanting to put all the pieces of her puzzle together here.

"No," she confessed. "No one appropriate. Certainly no one as impressive as you."

When she looked him up and down again with admiring eyes, Callum wasn't sure if he felt flattered or flustered. He'd never considered himself all that good-looking. He certainly wasn't in Clay's league.

Admittedly, his tall, broad-shouldered frame looked pretty good in the superbly tailored tux he'd bought when he was working in Milan last year. And as Clay had said, he did have a great tan at the moment.

Maybe his date had a yen for bronze and brawn.

Hell, he seriously hoped not. He was here to do a job, not be seduced by some female on the rebound, no matter how gorgeous she was. Damn, but he wished she'd stop looking at him like he was a cool beer and she'd just emerged from the Sahara Desert after a six-month trek.

As though reading his mind, she stopped the staring, but not before a quivery little shudder ran down her spine.

Who knew what she'd been thinking. It was probably best he didn't know. Nothing turned Callum on more than his date being turned on.

"I suppose I should fill you in on the total picture," she went on with a blessed return to the business at hand. "It'll make your job easier if you know a bit of background stuff."

True, he thought.

"The last time I went to a class reunion was five years ago. Unfortunately, it was just after I filed for divorce and I was a total wreck."

Callum's eyebrows lifted slightly. Divorced too, eh? She certainly didn't have much luck with men.

"I should never have gone," she muttered. "Certainly not alone. All I did was burst into tears all night. And I looked such a fright. I'd lost a lot of weight at the time. It was one of the worst nights of my life and the memory has haunted me ever since.''

Callum could well imagine. No one liked to look a fool, or a failure, in front of old school friends.

''I haven't been to a reunion since, but when the invitation came for this year's special ten-year reunion, I decided to go, just to show everyone that I'd really turned my life around. Unfortunately, I told the gossipy head of the organizing committee last week that I was bringing my new boyfriend. Fortunately, I didn't tell them his name, but I stupidly bragged a bit about how good-looking and successful he was.''

''I see,'' Callum murmured.

''Not entirely. There's more. There's this one girl, you see, who always hated me at school and got infinite pleasure out of witnessing the exhibition of myself I made at the last reunion. I guess she's the one I want to show most of all. She's hosting the party tonight at her multi-million dollar harborside mansion. She's married to Ted Billingsworth. You know...the communications tycoon.''

''Yeah, I've heard of him.'' From what he'd heard, Callum didn't like the sound of Ted Billingsworth. A womanizer from way back. Callum didn't think he'd be any kind of prize as a husband, unless all you wanted out of marriage was money.

''Actually, when Angus became my latest personal disaster, I almost wimped out and stayed away. But then I heard about *Gentleman Partners* and their lineup of handsome hunks for hire and I thought, what the hell? Go for it! So I did. And here you are,'' she finished up, her chin lifting in an attitude of spirited rebellion. "My own handsome hunk for the night."

What a girl, Callum thought. She had the kind of pick-yourself-up-off-the-floor courage he admired. If she hadn't also been highly emotional, sensitive, divorced and recently dumped, he might have asked her out for real.

"A hunk, anyway," he agreed with a modest smile. "I'm not sure about the handsome part."

"Are you kidding me? You're drop-dead gorgeous!" she exclaimed before looking shocked at herself. "Sorry. I didn't mean to gush. This is just so new to me. I mean, hiring a man for the night. But trust me, Beau, you are one *very* handsome man."

"Well, I'm happy you think so," he said. Yet he wasn't happy. Here he was, with a gorgeous girl who liked him and he couldn't lay a finger on her. Which was more than just a pity. It was downright frustrating.

It had been ages since Callum had had sex. Hawaii had been a total wipe-out where the ladies were concerned, the females who'd come on to him either being married, or desperately wanting to be. He'd been substituting surfing for sex for the last three months, and the result was one very nicely tanned but rather testy guy.

"When a colleague recommended you, I have to confess I was initially reluctant," Josie prattled on. "But Kay insisted."

Callum feared that his cover was about to be blown. "I've been hired by a colleague of yours in the past?"

"Actually, not Kay herself. It was her cousin. Cora."

"Cora," Callum repeated before realizing he was sounding like he'd been hired by so many women that they all blurred into one.

"You must remember Cora. She's a rally-car driver, which is a pretty unique occupation for a woman. You took her to an industry awards dinner not long back. She certainly remembers you. She simply raved to Kay over your looks and your performance."

"Really? And what performance, exactly, would that have been?"

Callum was astonished when she actually blushed. So! Madam wasn't *that* bold, not if his unintended double-entendre embarrassed her.

"You…er…pretended to be her boy-toy lover for the evening," she explained, her cheeks glowing. "To make her ex-husband jealous. You *must* remember. I was told it wasn't long ago."

"Oh yes…of course. Cora," he murmured, digesting this highly interesting piece of information. It seemed he was getting Clay out of the escort business just in time. That boy had no common sense at all. Boy-toy indeed! What next?

"I thought if you had no trouble pretending to be a forty-year-old woman's lover, then you'd have no trouble pretending to be mine."

"You're quite right," he agreed. "Pretending to be *your* boyfriend will be a piece of cake."

At this compliment, she blushed some more.

Ms. Josie Williams was an enigma all right, an intriguing mixture of daring and innocence.

"You ready to go then?" he asked. "My car's parked right outside."

"You know, I was thinking...I could easily call for a taxi. You might like to have a few drinks tonight. The beer and wine are sure to be laid on."

"No, ma'am, I never drink on the job." Now he sounded like a cop. A very pompous cop.

She smiled a stiff little smile. "I think you'd better call me Josie, don't you?"

"Yep. I think you could be right there. And you can call me Callum."

"Callum! But I thought your name was Beau?"

Callum knew he couldn't stand that name all night. He'd wince every time she said it. With Clay out of that agency tomorrow what did it matter what name he used tonight, as long as he kept up the pretense of being from *Gentlemen Partners.* He had to do that, otherwise there might be trouble, and that was what he was always trying to avoid. Trouble.

"Beau Grainger was a name I chose for my escort work," he explained. "Like a stage name. Frankly, I can't get used to it so I've decided to revert back to my real name. Which is Callum. Callum McCloud."

"Callum McCloud," she repeated, savoring his name as one might savor a sip of wine. Very thoughtfully. "Yes," she said, nodding. "That fits you better than Beau Grainger. *Much* better. I'll just get my purse and shawl and we'll get going." She turned away to walk toward a nearby hall stand, her body in motion threatening Callum's intention to keep strictly to his Gentleman Partner role tonight.

Frankly, he'd never been confronted by a more tempting sight in all his life. That curtain of gorgeous black hair swinging across her deliciously bare back brought seriously erotic images to mind. As did the split up the back of that long clinging red skirt, exposing great legs with shapely calves and narrow ankles.

Callum's gaze stayed glued to her as she picked up a beaded black shawl from the hall stand, and threw it around her beautifully bare shoulders with all the style and grace of a flamenco dancer. It was a sensual movement, with a sexually provocative garment, the shawl being transparent behind the beads.

Callum was glad Josie took her time, checking her hair in the mirror first as well as the contents of a black beaded purse, then extracting a set of keys from the hall stand drawer before turning back to face him. By then, he had his wayward body under stern control.

Still, it seemed the coming evening wasn't going to be the piece of cake he claimed it would be. Not unless he could have *this* piece of cake, and eat it too.

5

WHEN JOSIE FELT she could not delay any longer, she turned back to face him.

"Ready now," she said in what she hoped was a casual yet confident voice. In truth, she hadn't felt either casual or confident since she'd opened the front door and come face to face with a physical replica of her favorite fantasy lover.

Josie shrank from thinking back over the way she'd acted since that moment. The gobbling him up with her eyes. Her gushing over his looks, not to mention blushing over his perfectly innocent use of the word *performance*.

Of course, her wicked mind had immediately put a sexual connotation on it, after which her imagination had been off and running....

Her imagination had been off and running from the moment she'd set eyes on the man.

As she walked slowly back to where he was still standing in the front hall—looking oh so cool—Josie found it hard to believe her escort was only in his midtwenties. There was an air of masculine maturity about Callum McCloud that most young guys simply didn't have.

Still, most young guys weren't built like him. Neither did their marginally post-adolescent features have such definition. Josie really liked his strong, if somewhat sharp nose, his firmly sculpted mouth and determinedly macho jawline. She especially liked his hard blue eyes and outdoorsy tan.

His rugged good looks probably weren't to every girl's taste; hence his endearingly modest surprise that she thought him so handsome. But to her, he was the stuff her dreams were made of. Which meant she found him far too attractive for her to totally behave herself tonight.

But he's *supposed* to be your boyfriend, Josie, the voice of temptation whispered as her gaze took in his fantastic body once more, shown off to perfection in that fabulous black suit. It would be only natural for you to hold his hand sometimes, or his arm, or even snuggle right up to him.

And then there'd be the dancing!

Josie's heart quickened. There was sure to be music and dancing at some stage tonight. It was a party, after all.

The thought of his holding her close in his arms took Josie's breath away. Lord, but she was going to have some super fantasies during the course of this evening, that was for sure.

Suddenly, Amber and her crowd were far from Josie's mind as she recalled the fantastic fantasy which had swept her away at work the other day, where she'd hired a man for the night, not as an escort but as the kind of lover described in that magazine article.

What she wouldn't give for *that* scenario to come true!

But of course it wasn't going to. Despite his being her perfect dream man to look at, Callum McCloud was not here to fulfil her sexual fantasies. He was here to do the job she'd hired him for and which she should get her mind back onto, pronto, or risk making a bigger fool of herself than she had at the last reunion.

Chastened, Josie summoned up a polite smile and refrained from taking her pretend boyfriend's arm as she joined him.

"I just have to lock up," she said, glancing briefly up at him but carefully avoiding more than a fleeting contact with those sexy blue eyes. Looking into them too much was asking for trouble.

"Is this your house?" he inquired as she proceeded to lock the dead lock as well as the normal lock.

"Heavens, no, I could never afford a place like this. No, this is my parents' home. I'm house-sitting for them while they're overseas, doing Europe in six weeks flat. Silly time to go in November with winter on their doorstep, but my mother refused to go during peak tourist season. She hates crowds. It's a bit of a pain having to look after the garden and feed the goldfish every other day, but how could I refuse?" She smiled up at him.

"No brothers or sisters to help?" Callum asked her as she popped the keys into her black beaded evening purse then pulled the drawstring tight.

"No. Afraid not. I'm an only child. To be honest this house-sitting job hasn't been nearly as bad as I thought it would be. I've been sharing an old place at Milsons Point with a couple of girlfriends for nearly three years now and I think I must have needed a break. I always imagined that living alone would be awfully lonely, and perhaps it would be, in the long term. But at the moment, I quite like coming home to peace and quiet, with no one to interfere with whatever I want to do, or say.''

Too late, Josie realized she'd been staring up into his eyes for far too long, because all of a sudden, she found herself wallowing in a new fantasy where Callum brought her home tonight and simply didn't leave. Not for the whole time her parents were away. He'd be waiting for her every evening when she came home from work. Waiting and willing to do whatever she wanted him to do...

''I know exactly what you mean,'' he said ruefully. ''I like my own space. I would never live with anyone else.''

Josie almost laughed. Oh well. There went the chances of that little fantasy coming true. But as she'd accepted earlier, fantasies weren't meant to come true. Hence the word *fantasy*. They were make-believe. Fiction. Fun for the mind. The kind of fun no man could deny her.

Callum might not know it but he was going to give her a lot of that kind of fun tonight, and be damned with the reunion, and the likes of Amber and Brenda. Josie was sick of caring what people like them thought. She was also sick of worrying if she would ever meet Mr. Right and become Mrs. Right with a whole lot of little Rights running around. She was sick of *all* of her mission impossible wish list.

Tonight, she was going to settle for what was at hand, which was this gorgeously sexy guy whom she was paying big bucks to give her his undivided attention all evening, as well as pretend she was the love of his life.

Which reminded her. She'd have to find out some more about him. As much as she no longer wanted people like Amber and Brenda to shape her decisions in life or her potential for happiness, Josie still didn't want to look like a fool around them.

"What about you, Callum?" she asked as they walked companionably up the wide stone steps which led to the road—Josie had decided to leave any hand- or arm-holding till they arrived at the reunion, where she had a legitimate excuse for such intimacies. "Do you have any brothers or sisters?"

"I have one brother. Clay."

"And your parents?"

Callum shrugged. "My dad took off when I was six and my mother's dead. She died a few years back. Brain tumor."

"Oh!" Josie gasped, shock and sympathy mixing in her heart. "Oh, how sad. That must have been devastating for you and your brother."

"Yeah, it was," Callum agreed. But he didn't like to talk about it. What was the point? Nothing was going to bring her back.

Callum had a theory that talking about a problem or grief ad infinitum only made it worse. He had no patience with post-trauma counseling or that group therapy crap. Why dwell on pain and the reasons for it?

That was the trouble with the world these days. Everything was analyzed to death. Bad things happen. That's life. You get over it. End of story.

"I can't imagine what I'd do if my mother died like that," Josie said softly, before noting the clammed-up look on Callum's face.

Better get off that subject, Josie.

"Do you have a Sydney street directory in your car?" she asked.

"Sure do."

"Amber's place is in Elizabeth Bay. I've never been there before but I have the address written down and I'm pretty good at reading maps."

She was glad to see the muscles in his face relax into a smile. "An unusual talent in a female."

"I've inherited quite a few skills from my dad. I'm good at math, *and* maps."

"Clever as well as beautiful," Callum murmured. "So what do you do for a living, Josie?"

Josie opened her mouth to tell him when the sight of a red sports car by the sidewalk distracted her train of thought. Her eyes rounded at this amazing coincidence, because *all* of Josie's fantasy lovers drove red sports cars.

"Is…is that your car?" she asked, trying not to look too pleased.

"Well…yes. You have a problem with my car?"

"No, no, it's utterly gorgeous." Like you, she almost added, but stopped herself just in time. "Escort work must be very profitable."

"I didn't buy the car with escort money," he said brusquely before zapping the car unlocked, then opening the passenger door.

Josie tactfully refrained from asking him what he *had* bought it with. But she was curious. Since he was an aspiring but so far unsuccessful actor, she'd assumed he wasn't well off. Still, maybe he'd bought the car with money he'd inherited after his mother's death. Maybe she'd had a big life insurance policy. And maybe—a far more likely answer—he was up to his eyes in debt, living life in the fast lane on credit. That suit he was wearing was not cheap, and it fitted far too well to be rented.

Whatever, she'd obviously trodden on sensitive toes with her question and decided not to pursue the subject, or ask him too many other personal questions, only what was strictly necessary.

When he got in the car, she decided to answer *his* earlier question, the one he'd asked before their conversation had turned to the awkward subject of sports cars and money.

"I run my own property styling company," she told him. "It's called *Property Presentation Perfect.* PPP for short. I started it up a couple of years back."

His hand lifted from where he'd been about to turn the ignition, his sideward glance showing surprise. "That's impressive," he said, "for one so young."

She laughed. "Not as impressive as it sounds. PPP has two whole employees so far. Myself and Kay. She's my interior decorator and utterly brilliant, I might add. I'm the business manager, accountant, salesperson and general dogsbody. Of course, we do contract out tradespeople as well…when we can afford them. We did quite well the first year but lately, it's been a real struggle. Still…we'll make it. Eventually."

"I'm sure you will," he said, and smiled over at her. "You're a winner. No doubt about that."

Was it his calling her a winner, or the way his eyes glittered as they raked over her? Whatever, Josie's earlier impression that Callum looked upon her strictly as an escorting job suddenly flew out the car window.

He fancied her. Maybe not as much as she fancied him, but enough to put a different slant on the evening ahead.

Kay had stressed that *Gentlemen Partners* had a strict no-sex policy, but what happened if one of their handsome young escorts was genuinely attracted to a client? What if sparks flew when they looked at each other, as had just happened? What if the chemistry between them could not be denied?

Handsome young men these days didn't deny themselves when it came to sex. Josie couldn't see Callum being any different, regardless of his looking and acting a little more mature than most. If he thought she wanted him—and he had to with the way her eyes were glued to his at this very moment—then he was sure to make a pass at the end of the night.

Heat spread through Josie at the prospect.

"The street directory is in here," he said, breaking off eye contact to lean over her right thigh and press open the glove compartment.

Josie stiffened, showing her exactly what would happen if he *did* make a genuine pass at the end of the evening. She'd freeze. That's what. She'd been living in her fantasy world so long that the real world of sex frightened her.

The brutal truth was she probably wouldn't have

gone to bed with Angus the other night. She'd had trouble going to bed with men ever since her divorce. She always worried that it would be a colossal failure again, and inevitably, it was.

Josie was finally faced with the fact that the fault might not have been entirely the man's every time over the past few years. Maybe she was her own worst enemy. She *expected* to feel nothing remotely like the way she felt in her fantasies, and that's exactly what she always felt. Nothing.

Unless she could change her attitude, then she was doomed to living her real life in a sexual void. Perhaps this was her chance to change, with this virtual stranger. Callum had no preconceptions about her. She was whatever she presented to him tonight. She was a blank canvas and she could paint whatever picture pleased her. And what pleased her was to be a confident outgoing sexy woman who knew what she wanted in life and wasn't afraid to go after it.

This wasn't at odds with the picture she'd already presented to him. She would just continue as she'd started, but with more boldness, more confidence, more daring. There would be no more freezing. No shrinking back. No thinking negative thoughts.

Josie vowed not to do *anything* tonight which might stop Callum from making a pass at the end of the evening.

"Thanks," she purred, lifting the directory out and placing it on her lap before shutting the glove compartment door again. "You are just so nice. But I suppose all the women who hire you tell you that."

Again, he looked faintly embarrassed, which she thought was *so* sweet.

"I have to confess I do have a hundred percent record where that's concerned. But that's my job, Josie. To be nice to my clients, and to do whatever they want me to do."

Oh, good, she thought. And smiled over at him.

6

OH, OH, CALLUM THOUGHT when he saw that siren's smile coming his way. You made a big mistake complimenting her back there, buddy, not to mention looking at her like the big bad wolf sizing up Little Red Riding Hood.

But, hey, he was only human. She was just so damned delicious. Not only that, she fancied him. Maybe not as much as he fancied her—no one could fancy anyone as much as that—but enough to be a pain in the butt, not to mention in another part of his body.

Callum silently cursed Clay for putting him in this unenviable position. Then cursed himself for letting his guard slip.

Impossible now to revert to his earlier, more reserved attitude. She'd think he was weird. Besides, he was supposed to be her boyfriend for the night. Anyone who was Josie's boyfriend would not be acting cool and distant around her. He'd be white-hot horny and all over her like a rash.

No, he'd have to continue being "nice," for want of a better word, and hope that his willpower and common sense came to his rescue at the end of the evening and not let him do anything *really* stupid. Because let's face it, buddy, Josie was not one-night-stand material any more than she was girlfriend material. She was on the rebound and vulnerable with a capital *V*! Taking her to bed tonight could mean trouble in the morning. The kind of trouble he'd vowed never to countenance again.

Her living all alone in that lovely big house, however, did not help Callum's resolve to be sensible. It was sure to have lots of lovely big bedrooms full of lovely big beds....

He had to stop this!

Callum cleared his throat, if not his mind, then revved the engine.

"We'd better make tracks to your reunion," he said curtly as he angled the car away from the sidewalk. "I'll need directions once we're through the Harbour Tunnel, so study up. We don't want to get lost." With a bit of luck that should keep her quiet for a while.

It didn't. If Callum didn't know better he'd have thought she was on something. She chatted all the way to the Harbour Bridge, telling him all sorts of things about herself and her family, things she said he should know if they were really dating.

Frankly, she told him more personal details than were required on a form for a bank loan. Which was just about everything you'd done from birth to what you had for breakfast that morning.

He found out she'd trained to be an accountant, and had married young, straight out of university. The marriage had lasted eighteen months. Eighteen *ghastly* months, she said with feeling, but didn't elaborate further, though it was clear she was the one who'd asked for a divorce.

Callum didn't even try to speculate on why. He was just glad she hadn't had children. Children were always the ones who suffered most in a divorce.

On leaving her husband, she'd also left the accounting firm where they'd worked together in the auditing section. She returned home to live for a while, totally depressed, hardly eating a bite and generally being a misery. It was during this skinny, bedraggled, poor-little-me phase that she'd gone to that other class reunion five years ago and made a big fool of herself.

Shortly after her twenty-fourth birthday, she'd pulled herself together, got herself a job in a large accounting firm based in North Sydney and moved out of the house, hopping from apartment to apartment over the next eighteen months before ending up sharing her present place at Milsons Point with two working girls she felt she could live with. Their names were Deb and Lisa, both with office jobs in the city and heading for the big three-oh.

Around this time Josie quit her job—after being moved into the auditing section—and went to work for her father, who was an importer of furniture and household goods and had a warehouse and offices in Annandale. She helped with his books and started up a furniture rental section, making use of the furniture and other decorative items which had sustained slight damage in the shipping and couldn't be sold, except at a discount. Renting them out was much more profitable than selling them at a reduced price.

It was the success of this section, and meeting up

with an interior decorator she respected and liked which gave Josie the idea of starting up the property stylist company, which, as she'd told Callum earlier, was going through a really rough patch. Apparently, the success or demise of PPP rested on this apartment they were redecorating at the moment and which went up for auction the following Saturday, a week from today.

"If it sells for well over the reserve," she raved on, "we'll make a bundle of money and get loads more work. If it doesn't, then I'm not sure we'll survive. I could keep things going if I don't take any salary and go back to living at home permanently, but I don't really want to do that. My parents are lovely people but they make me feel like a child sometimes. I'm too old for that. I'm my own boss now and I like it that way."

Callum knew exactly what she meant.

Her conversation didn't turn toward him till he was whizzing through the Harbour Tunnel. "I'm sorry, Callum, but we'll have to invent a profession for you other than actor," she said with a slightly sheepish sideward glance. "I need my boyfriend to be doing something really successful. Do you mind?"

"No," he said succinctly.

"You haven't done anything on television that anyone would remember, have you?"

"No." It crossed Callum's mind that it was just as well Clay hadn't been her escort tonight. Someone at the reunion was sure to have seen him in that television soap. Once seen, Clay's was not a face one forgot.

"I wonder what you could be, then?" she mused

aloud. "Not a doctor. You don't look like a doctor. Or a dentist. And certainly not an accountant." She actually shuddered when she said this.

"An engineer," he suggested smoothly.

"An engineer!" She beamed over at him. "What a great idea. And it really suits you. You actually look the engineering type."

"Do I?" He couldn't help but smile.

"Absolutely. And it would explain that gorgeous tan. So what kind of engineering do you do, Callum?" she asked in a delighted and somewhat mischievous tone.

"Big construction work," he said truthfully. "Sky-scrapers. Bridges. Shopping malls. I work for INCON. It's a large American company who have offices in every major city of the world. I'm one of their trouble-shooters. Don't stay in one place for long. I was in London, Paris and Milan last year. This year I've been in Bangkok, Tokyo and Hawaii. It's been my Pacific year. My contract allows me to fly home to Sydney every few months for some R & R, which is when and how I met you."

"Wow! What an imagination! Still, I suppose that's what makes a good actor."

"It helps." Clay's imagination was extraordinary. He used to tell his friends horror stories when they came to sleep over when he was a little kid. They often had nightmares for weeks afterward.

"There could be one hurdle to your suggestion, however."

"What?"

"Aren't you a little young to have done all that?" Josie quizzed him.

"No," he returned with a straight face. "I am thirty, after all."

Her head jerked around to stare at him for a couple of seconds. And then she laughed. "But of course! How clever of you. No one there will know your real age. And you could easily pass for thirty. Oh, this is fabulous. And such fun."

"It is, isn't it," he agreed with a grin, finally putting aside his concern over how the evening might end and just enjoying it as it came along. He'd worry about later on, later on.

"How long, exactly, have we been dating?" came her next eager question just as they zoomed out of the Harbour Tunnel, catching a glimpse of the city before plunging underground again into the Eastern Distributor.

"What did you say about your boyfriend to the people running this reunion?" he returned.

"I said I was bringing my *new* boyfriend, which implies a pretty recent relationship."

Callum decided he should stick to the truth as much as possible, because *his* truth was that he was hopeless as an actor. And unlike Clay's wild imagination, his was more limited.

"Then let's just say recently. We don't have to be specific."

"Okay, but they're sure to ask where we met. That's a very common question."

"How about a mutual friend set us up on a blind date?"

"Oh, yes, that's good. That's the sort of thing Kay might do."

"Kay…" Callum searched his mind for what part Kay played in Josie's life. There'd been a lot of names mentioned. "Is she one of your roommates or the interior decorator?"

"Kay's the interior decorator. Deb and Lisa are my roommates."

"Right. Got it this time. Now tell me what exit to use to get to Elizabeth Bay."

7

AMBER'S HOUSE MET every one of Josie's expectations. It was palatial and pretentious, a mock Italian villa in a pale terra-cotta color with columned porticoes, acres of marble steps and a huge stone fountain in the front garden which sported several naked statues and a lot of expensive lighting.

Some of Josie's earlier nerves returned at the sight of the place, sending a quiver down her spine. There she'd been, pretending to herself that Amber couldn't rattle her anymore. Faint hope that was!

"Strange venue for a class reunion," Callum muttered as he was waved to a halt at the open gates by a uniformed security guard.

Callum wound his window down. "Yes?"

"Invitation, please, sir," came the curt request, upon which Callum glanced over at Josie.

A nasty little feeling started to crawl through her stomach. "I...I didn't know I had to bring it with me."

The security guard, who would not have been out of place as a captain in any secret police, bent to give her a cold glare. "That request was made on every invitation, ma'am. I'm to check each one presented against the list of names I've been given."

"My name is Josie Williams. Check your list. I know I'm on it."

He checked the list. "Yes, that name is here, but that's beside the——"

"I can show you my driving license," she interrupted and pulled open the drawstring of her evening purse before groaning. "Oh, no, I can't. I didn't bring that with me, either. I didn't think I'd need it."

He gave her another highly skeptical look. "No matter, ma'am. I can't let you through till I've spoken with Mrs. Billingsworth, anyway. I've been given very strict instructions to let her know if anyone arrives without an invitation. Apparently, last time she held a party here, there were several very undesirable gate-crashers."

The guard stepped back from the car and whipped a cell phone off his belt. Soon he was talking to someone in a low voice but Josie couldn't hear what was said.

"Charming fellow," Callum muttered dryly.

"I know my invitation had no such request on it," Josie insisted as her stomach churned. "I would have seen it."

"I agree with you," Callum said. "Frankly, this whole situation smells fishy. Tell me, would your old classmate go to these lengths just to embarrass you?"

Although shocked at the idea, Josie had to admit that she would.

"Then don't give her the satisfaction of being in any way upset, Josie. Laugh it off."

"I've always found it very hard to do that." Especially where Amber was concerned.

"Then learn. And learn fast. Because if I'm right, our esteemed hostess will shortly be making a personal appearance. What would be the point of all this if she doesn't see your supposed humiliation for herself?"

The guard returned, his manner and voice as rude as before. "You are to proceed over to the bottom of the front steps where the parking valet is stationed. He will direct you to a spot where you are to wait till Mrs. Billingsworth can come and vouch for you personally. Under no circumstances are you to leave your vehicle."

"Yes, sir!" Callum ground out as he drove on round the grand, gravel-covered circular driveway, his face like rapidly setting concrete. Gone was the supercool, super-suave escort. In place was a man having difficulty holding on to his temper.

Josie's heart quickened in time with her revolving insides. "What...what are you going to do? I thought you said I was to laugh this off."

Callum was looking far from amused. "That was before," he grated. "This is now."

Callum stopped his car right in front of the parking valet, who was speaking on his cell phone. Probably to the security guard, because he looked shocked when Callum immediately climbed out from behind the wheel.

"Hey! You there!" he called out over the hood of the low-slung sports car. "You're not supposed to leave your vehicle till Mrs. Billingsworth gets here."

Josie watched a grim-faced Callum stride around the front of his car and mount the bottom of the many steps which led up to the house. He totally ignored the parking valet—whom he towered over by six inches—and bent down to open the passenger door.

"Get out, Josie," he commanded, holding his hand out to her. "We're going inside. And if that idiot behind me tries to stop us then he'll wish he hadn't."

Josie gnawed at her bottom lip as she took Callum's hand then swung her feet out of the car. He hoisted her to her feet in somewhat of a rush, his white-knuckled fingers showing a marked degree of suppressed anger.

"Oh dear," she said breathlessly, fearful that tonight was going to be over before it had begun. She had visions of ending up in the local police station with Callum charged with assault. "Please don't cause a scene, Callum. It's not worth it."

"I'll cause more than a scene if this crap goes on much longer," he muttered as he cupped her elbow and turned her toward the mountain of steps. "And you *are* worth it," he finished up with a reproachful glance which Josie found tremendously endearing.

More and more Callum resembled her dream man. Not only sexy but strong and authoritative.

"Here. Park the car," he said, tossing his keys toward the valet who caught them with a nervous fumble.

"And be careful," Callum snapped. "If I come out and find even the tiniest dent, then I'm going to sue you and your employer. Do I make myself clear?"

The valet, who had to be all of eighteen, flushed a bright red. "Yes, sir. I'll be most careful."

"Good. And if you have any trouble with your bullying buddy on the gate over letting us dare get out of our car and go inside, then you can refer him to me and I'll straighten him out. The name's McCloud. Callum McCloud.''

''Yes, sir, Mr. McCloud!''

''Come along, darling,'' Callum said with obviously gritted teeth as he urged her up the steps. ''We've been delaycd by this nonsense long enough.''

''Wow, that was seriously impressive,'' she whispered. ''And I liked the darling bit.''

''You're paying me to be impressive. And to pretend to be your boyfriend. No boyfriend worth his salt would put up with his lady being insulted like that.''

''Not many boyfriends these days take on the role of protector. They say we girls demanded equality and shouldn't complain when we get it.''

''In that case call me old-fashioned because I still believe a boyfriend's role is to be his girlfriend's champion. As well as other things, of course.''

''Your girlfriend must be suitably appreciative.''

Josie already suspected he didn't have a steady girlfriend—what girlfriend would want her boyfriend doing a job like this?—but she felt compelled to find out for sure.

''They usually are,'' he returned cryptically.

''They?'' Good Lord, was he admitting to having several going at once?

''I've had a few.''

Josie suppressed a sigh of relief. Clearly, he was referring to the past. ''I don't doubt it. What about right now?'' No point in not making *absolutely* sure.

He threw her a look which suggested he knew exactly what she was doing. ''I'm between girlfriends at the moment. And I'm not on the lookout for one. As delightful as you are, Josie, I am only here doing a job, the one you hired me for. Don't take anything I say or do this evening in a personal fashion—which includes calling you darling just now—or meaning I want any more from you than what we will share tonight.''

Josie couldn't help feeling momentarily crushed with this announcement, but in keeping with her new self, she resolved not to give up just yet. He thought her delightful. That was a start, wasn't it? And he was between girlfriends. The coast was clear.

Full steam ahead, girl!

''That's all right,'' she said blithely, well aware that men hated women who acted desperate. ''I can live with that. But given that I'm paying you to do what I want tonight, then I'd like you to keep on calling me darling. It had just the right ring to it.'' It had also felt deliciously intimate and sexy.

His smile was wry, but resigned. ''In that case darling it will be. The client is always right.''

Josie beamed, her earlier good humor and positive attitude fully restored.

But her smile—and her confidence—faded when Amber suddenly appeared at the top of the steps, glowering down at them and looking every inch the ravishing rich bitch she'd always been.

Josie said a rude word under her breath and Callum followed the direction of her gaze.

''Our esteemed hostess?'' he quizzed quietly.

''Who else,'' Josie muttered through gritted teeth.

''Excellent. I've been looking forward to meeting

Mrs. Billingsworth. Now remember what I told you, darling. *Smile*. And when you're not smiling, *laugh*.''

After pulling a face at him, she plastered a saccharine smile on her face. "How's that?"

"Marginally better. But if I catch you letting that woman get under your skin, we're out of here. Okay?"

"Okay," Josie said, thinking she wouldn't mind getting out of here right now. But she had to stay, firstly to put Amber's ghost to rest once and for all. But also because if Callum took her home now, he was sure to just drop her off and leave. If she stayed here, she at least had an excuse to touch him, and flirt with him, and hopefully dance with him.

Josie shivered with renewed erotic anticipation.

"No need to be afraid," Callum said, misinterpreting her little shudder. "You have me by your side. Remember me? I'm Callum, your boyfriend, your champion. I won't let anything bad happen to you tonight, Josie. I promise."

Josie looked up into those strong sexy blue eyes of his and wondered what he would do if she just *asked* him to stay with her tonight. No strings, of course. She could see he was at a no-strings time in his life. That's why he'd warned her about not wanting a girlfriend right now. She could offer a one-night stand. No emotional involvement. No promises of any kind. Surely he'd go for that. He was only twenty-four, for pity's sake. A modern guy in his sexual prime.

"Time to face your nemesis, darling," he said, and she almost laughed.

Because Amber wasn't really her nemesis anymore. *Sex* was.

It was a shame she couldn't tell him that, but she couldn't. He'd run a mile. Men didn't like neurotic females with heavy emotional garbage, certainly not a young no-strings kind of guy like Callum.

As for herself, there was no use pretending she'd have the courage to ask him straight out to take her to bed when he took her home. No, her only chance of getting Callum into her bed tonight was if he thought it was his idea.

Which meant she had to seduce him. If she could.

When she sighed, Callum glared at her again. "Stop that sighing and keeping smiling," he ordered curtly. "Or we turn around and walk back down these steps right now."

Josie stopped sighing and kept smiling.

8

In a superficial and strictly visual fashion, Amber Billingsworth had to be the most beautiful woman Callum had ever set eyes on. She was perfect. Perfect hair. Perfect face. Perfect figure. And she was dressed as only the wife of a multimillionaire could afford to dress, very expensively and no doubt exclusively, in a slender and low-cut gold gown which screamed: designer label. Gold and diamonds decorated her honey-colored flesh from every vantage point. Neck. Ears. Wrists. Fingers. She was ablaze with her wealth.

But despite all this in-your-face splendor, nothing could hide the malice behind those coldly beautiful green eyes, or the shock which flashed briefly across her face when she saw Josie being escorted up toward the house, instead of having stayed obediently in the car.

"Who's that?" he asked Josie when a woman in pale pink came to stand by the golden queen's side.

"Brenda. She's the organizer of this do and Amber's devoted slave."

"Aah."

"Josie!" Amber exclaimed once they were too close for her to ignore. "So it really *is* you. Security said someone using your name was trying to get in without an invitation. I told them to hold whoever it was till I saw this gatecrasher for myself, because I couldn't believe you'd forgotten to bring your invitation. After all, it was clearly marked on the RSVP section to bring the invitation with you tonight. Josie usually has a memory second to none, doesn't she, Brenda?''

"What? Oh yes, yes indeed," Brenda agreed.

Brenda was not an unattractive girl up close, Callum noted, though a little colorless. No competition for the golden queen, of course, whereas Josie with her striking dark looks and simple but stunningly sexy red dress would give her a real run for her money.

"But of course that was back in our school days," Amber swept on. "Maybe Josie's much-heralded photographic memory is not quite so brilliant anymore. Or maybe she was just a brilliant cheat back then," she added with a nasty little laugh.

Callum felt Josie stiffen. When he pinched her elbow, she laughed back. "Very funny, Amber. I see your talent for teasing hasn't lessened with the years. But to set the record straight, my invitation had absolutely nothing on it about having to bring it with me tonight."

Callum almost clapped his approval. Brenda looked startled, and Amber herself feigned a patently false confusion.

"Really?" she said. "Are you sure? How odd."

"Yes, isn't it?" Josie reiterated, but in a wonderfully carefree manner. "Just a little tip, Amber. I wouldn't hire that security guard again if I were you. He was really very rude."

"Oh dear, I am *so* sorry, but I guess he was just doing his job. And perhaps not very well," she added with a brittle smile, "since you were supposed to stay in your car till I came."

"Blame me for that," Callum said, deciding it was high time he stepped in. "I could see there must have been some mix-up so I took matters into my own hands and just brought Josie in. I thought I'd save you the embarrassment, Mrs. Billingsworth, of discovering that two of your guests had been treated so shabbily."

"Did you?" Callum felt the full force of Amber's snobbish and overbearing personality as her eyes locked with his. "How thoughtful of you. I presume you must be Josie's new boyfriend, the one she never stopped raving about to Brenda the other night."

"Did you rave about me, darling?" he said, giving Josie an intimate little squeeze. "How sweet."

"Why don't you introduce us, Josie?" Amber commanded imperiously, "so I can put a name to your knight in shining armor?"

"The name's Callum, Mrs. Billingsworth," Callum said before Josie was compelled to obey this appalling creature. "Callum McCloud."

"I do hope you're not going to call me Mrs. Billingsworth all night," she said sharply. "My name is Amber. And this is Brenda."

He nodded coolly toward Brenda, still not sure if she'd been in on that invitation business.

"Amber, oh, Amber!" a new arrival trilled from behind them, giving Callum the opportunity to rescue Josie from Amber's poisonous company for a while. He could well understand why she had felt the need to hire him for tonight. To have shown up here without a boyfriend would have played into this bitch's hands perfectly.

Amber scowled at having to leave her prey, even for a second, though she recovered quickly to flash them all an apologetic I'd-much-rather-be-with-you smile. "Have to go, I'm afraid," she purred toward Callum. "Duty calls. Brenda, take Callum and Josie inside and show Josie where to put her shawl and purse. I'll be with you shortly."

"Yes, Amber," Brenda said like some robot, programmed to obey Amber without question.

Callum didn't know whether to be angry with the woman, or sorry for her.

"You haven't been to Amber's house before, have you, Josie?" Brenda said as she led them across the wide marble portico. "It's absolutely fabulous. It cost millions, of course. Then again, Amber's husband is worth *billions*."

"So I've heard," Josie replied casually. "Is he here tonight?"

"Unfortunately, no. Ted had to go to an important business dinner and couldn't make it."

Callum smothered a snigger. A business dinner on a Saturday night? Maybe, but not very likely. Still, there was always a price to be paid for marrying money.

"What about you, Brenda?" Josie asked. "Is your husband here tonight?"

Brenda looked uncomfortable with the question. "Actually, no. Amber said I'd have enough to do looking after everyone without worrying about John.

And to be honest, John doesn't get along all that well with Amber.''

Surprise, surprise, Callum thought dryly.

"This way…" Brenda opened one of the mansion-size front doors and waved them inside.

The house was as huge inside as it had looked from the outside. Callum could have fitted his terraced house in Glebe into the foyer alone. It reminded him of one particular skyscraper he'd worked on in Chicago. Built strictly for show, the whole place was all glitz and no soul, the function of its huge foyer no more than a monument to some tycoon's ego, an over-the-top display of wealth and bad taste.

Like this place.

Mock Corinthian columns were spaced at intervals over the cream marble floor. Massive crystal chandeliers hung from the domed ceiling and elaborate gilt-framed mirrors covered the ornately papered walls, providing endless reflections.

Obviously, Amber and her husband liked to look at themselves a lot.

"There's a cloakroom and ladies' room over here where all the girls have put their things," Brenda informed them as she veered to the left between two of the columns. "There a men's room opposite, if you wish to use it," she told Callum.

"Thanks. No need as yet. I'll wait for you over here, darling." And letting Josie's arm go, he walked toward where the foyer ended in a semicircular railing, beyond which he could hear party sounds.

Callum peered down into a sunken living area whose ballroom-size space was extended even farther through open French doors onto a covered back terrace. More steps led from the terrace down to a pool which looked like the one in the grounds of Hadrian's Palace.

Callum had visited the ruins of Hadrian's Palace when he'd been working in Rome last year, and been blown away by the whole place, but especially the once-magnificent pool. Surrounded by statues and columns, it had been designed to impress, and not for swimming. A guide had told him it was mainly used as a setting for the famous general's outdoor banquets. Callum imagined Amber's pool had a similar function as an impressive backdrop, rather than a source of fun or exercise. He couldn't imagine anyone actually diving in and disturbing the lakelike surface. He half expected to see swans gliding by at any moment.

Callum suspected that pool parties weren't high on Amber's agendas. Her hair might get messed up! No, the golden queen obviously preferred more formal indoor gatherings where overdressed guests stood around in stiff little groups, pretending they were having a good time, like the people below.

Fifty or so guests were already doing just that while several waiters circulated with silver trays, presenting a selection of drinks and dainty finger food. No one had dared to sit and lounge back on the brocade-covered sofas, and the chat was very subdued for a reunion of women.

As Callum stood there, listening to the innocuous background music and watching the men getting tucked into the free drink—probably out of boredom—he began to regret not taking Josie's suggestion of a taxi. He could have done with a drink himself. At the same time, perhaps it was fortuitous he was forced to stick to juice. He had to have his wits about him to protect Josie from Amber's poison-tipped verbal darts, which he was pretty sure hadn't stopped for the evening. On top of that, once alcohol did its trick of lessening his defences and heightening his libido, he would have no chance of resisting Josie's considerable attractions at the end of evening.

No…as dull as it seemed, it was best he stay stone cold sober. It might also be a good idea to watch Josie's alcoholic consumption as well. In his experience, alcohol—especially expensive champagne—had been known to turn even the most uptight virgin into a candidate for the seductress-of-the month award. The last thing he needed was for Josie to start seriously seducing him. Flirting he could handle, but anything more could be downright dangerous.

A flash of red caught the corner of his eye and he turned to watch Josie—minus the black shawl—walk toward him in that incredible red dress. Talk about poetry in motion.

Down, boy, he muttered to his nether regions.

Perversely, once she was close enough, Callum was unable to resist slipping an arm around Josie's waist and drawing her close to his side. Her face showed initial surprise but then undiluted pleasure as she sank willingly against him.

"Goodness, Brenda," Josie exclaimed on finally glancing away from him and down over the railing at the crowd below. "Is that Marie Robbins over there, wearing that sexy blue dress? It can't be. But yes, it is. My, hasn't she lost some weight. And she's dyed her hair red. Marie. Oh, Marie!'' Josie called out, and the girl with bright red hair glanced up.

''Josie!'' she squealed. ''Look everyone, it's Josie!''

They all looked, first at Josie and then at Callum. Brenda, Callum noted, kept glancing over her shoulder with trepidation on her face.

''Come down here, Josie,'' Marie invited, ''and tell us what you've been up to since we last saw you. Whatever it is, it's agreeing with you.''

''You ought to talk,'' Josie countered. ''You look fabulous.''

''I do, don't I?'' the redhead preened.

Josie turned back to Callum, her lovely eyes gleaming with happiness. ''Come on, I want to introduce you to all my classmates.''

''I'm totally at your disposal tonight, darling,'' he said, not without some irony in his voice.

Josie looked even more pleased, though Brenda looked even more wretched, hanging back when they began to walk to the nearby steps.

''Coming?'' Callum asked Brenda out of sheer devilment.

''Yes. No.'' Her face was stricken by the awful burden of making a decision for herself. ''I...I think I'd better wait here for Amber. I don't know what's keeping her.'' And she threw an anguished glance at the empty doorway.

''I'm sure she'll be here soon,'' Callum remarked dryly. A couple *had* come in while the girls had been in the cloakroom, but no Amber. Callum wouldn't mind betting she was ticking off the security guard for not enforcing her instructions.

"Do come with us, Brenda," Josie suggested warmly. "Amber might be ages. Besides, I need you to put names to some of these faces. It looks like there's been a lot of changes over the past five years. I don't recognize half the people here. And I'm not talking about the men!"

Brenda gave a small rueful laugh. "That's the pot calling the kettle black. Do you know how different you look tonight from the woman who came to the reunion five years ago? You looked like something the cat dragged in. And you cried so much, it was embarrassing."

Callum was pleased when Josie threw back her head and laughed. "I did, didn't I?"

"But just look at you now," Brenda went on, her tone a mixture of admiration and envy. "You're absolutely gorgeous. And so obviously happy."

"I have everything to be happy about," Josie replied with a nonchalant shrug.

"Yes, I can see that," Brenda said, and threw Callum a smile which was more sad than jealous.

Now Callum did feel sorry for Brenda. It was obvious that hanging around the likes of Amber wasn't doing her self-esteem any good. That bitch seemed to have a detrimental effect on even the strongest girl's ego. Take Josie, for instance. She hadn't seen Amber for five years but just the thought of meeting up with her again was enough to give her the frights.

But Josie had been splendid tonight so far, Callum thought. After an initial quake or two on arriving, she'd really stood up for herself. She was even being nice to Brenda, which was generous of her considering Brenda must have known something about that invitation business.

There was no doubt about it. Josie was a beautiful girl both inside and out, a far cry from the likes of Amber who, despite her outer beauty, was full of spite and pettiness and jealousy, a lot like the wicked queen in Snow White who couldn't bear for anyone to be fairer, or smarter, or even nicer.

"Sorry to have been so long."

Speak of the devil, Callum thought as the three of them whirled to find Amber right behind them.

"You know I've been wondering what it was that was so different about you, Josie," she swept on, her venomous smile indicating that another comment was on the way. "You've had a boob job, haven't you?"

"A *boob* job?" Josie looked momentarily shocked before chuckling with amusement. "Don't be ridiculous, Amber. If I'd had a boob job I'd have C-cups like yours."

Callum knew she hadn't meant that Amber had had a boob job. But it came out that way.

"I've just put on some much-needed weight," Josie elaborated, oblivious, it seemed, of Amber's fury.

"But you do your I-must-I-must-improve-my-bust exercises religiously every morning, darling," Callum added mischievously, giving Josie's waist another intimate little squeeze.

"You're *living* together?" Brenda said in startled tones. "You didn't tell me that the other night, Josie."

"We're not actually living together," Callum

jumped in. "It's just that since we met, we seem to end up spending every night together. The truth is I simply can't resist her."

"So how long have you two been going out exactly?" Amber asked with hard eyes.

Callum felt Josie stiffen slightly by his side.

But she didn't need to worry. He was ready for Amber.

"Oh, no, no, Amber," Josie surprised him by returning blithely. "We're not going to reveal all about our romance more than once. And Marie and the others are waiting down there, eager to ask all those same questions. Come on, everyone, let's go mingle."

"Magnificent," he whispered admiringly as he steered her down the steps.

"I hope you haven't forgotten that engineering biography you told me," she whispered back.

"Not a word of it." Hard to forget the truth. "Don't worry. I won't put a foot wrong."

Not during the party, anyway. He had no guarantees for later, however, when he took her home. He had an awful feeling he was going to put more than a foot wrong then. More likely his whole damned body!

9

CALLUM WAS a truly brilliant actor, Josie concluded. He certainly hadn't put a foot wrong. He even sounded like he'd actually been to all those foreign cities where he said he'd worked as a troubleshooter. He also managed to bring her own new career direction into the conversation, making her feel so good. In his hands, PPP sounded like a highly successful and innovative company which she ran with great flair.

Amber had been left floundering by the news of their personal and professional successes. When she hadn't been able to find anything to exploit or criticize, she'd flounced off, claiming she had to see to the buffet supper. And perhaps she did, but in her haste to depart, she didn't demand that Brenda go with her, which was odd.

Once she was gone, Callum had taken the opportunity to ask Brenda to change the music to something they could dance to. She'd been very hesitant at first, but surrendered to peer group pressure in the end, and now Josie was where she'd wanted to be all night, wrapped in Callum's strong arms, her own arms wound around his neck, their bodies swaying to a very seductive beat.

He'd steered her onto the terrace to dance, a highly

romantic setting with a star-studded sky above, and that Hollywood style pool down below. There were a few other couples dancing nearby, but not close enough to overhear their conversation.

"I was just thinking what a very good actor you are," she complimented him warmly. Hard not to do everything warmly, being so close to Callum.

"Pretending to be your boyfriend is not a difficult job, Josie."

"I was thinking more of the way you never slipped up with your story. You had an answer for everything. And it really seemed like you'd lived in all those cities."

"That wasn't all make-believe. I've done quite a bit of traveling."

"You mean you *were* in Europe last year?"

"Yes."

"Heavens! No wonder you haven't made it as an actor yet. You can't have had any time to go for auditions. You have to stay put in one city to succeed, Callum."

He smiled. "Don't you worry about me. I'll be fine."

"Do you have a private income, is that it?"

"Why do you ask that?"

"Well…you travel. You drive a snazzy car and that suit didn't come cheap."

"You're right. It didn't. I got it in Milan and it cost a bomb. But no, I don't have a private income. You've heard the expression of working your way around the world? Well, that's what I've done."

"Wow. I haven't done any traveling at all. So are you going to go overseas again in the near future?"

"Yes. Soon. You know, you're beginning to sound like Amber. What's with the questions all of a sudden?"

"Sorry. Just curious."

"A dangerous thing, curiosity."

A dangerous thing, dancing with *you,* she could have told him. She was talking to stop her imagination from starting up; to stop the X-rated thoughts which were threatening to creep in; to stop seeing him starring in every one of those fantasies she'd read about today, with her in the co-starring role.

Too late. She shouldn't have stopped talking.

With a resigned sigh, Josie closed her eyes and sank farther against him, lifting and winding her arms more tightly around his neck, the action rubbing her already erect nipples against the hard wall of his chest.

He tensed, and she was sure he was going to say something, or push her away. But he didn't. He responded by winding his left arm more tightly around her back and sliding his right hand down over the swell of her buttocks, spreading his fingers then using the pressure of his outsplayed palm to meld her lower body to his.

Suddenly, it wasn't any fantasy world which was galvanizing Josie's brain, but stark reality, the reality of Callum's erection rubbing against her stomach.

A wave of heat flooded Josie's body from her toes up. He wanted her. Quite a lot, by the feel of things. He wasn't just being nice to her because she'd paid him to. Penises didn't lie. Or fake. They reacted personally and primally.

Josie felt very primal herself, all a sudden. And intensely turned on. Amazingly, there was no fear in her. Nothing but naked desire and the most driving need to feel his flesh not on her outside but deep inside. She didn't seem to care that they were not alone. She would have let him lift her dress and do it right then and there if he'd wanted to.

The thought of him doing just that excited her unbearably.

"Callum," she whispered breathlessly, moving her hips against his in the most provocative way.

He swore, then jerked back to arm's length.

"Hell, Josie, if you keep this up I'll end up getting arrested for ravishing you right here on this very terrace."

"Is that a threat, or a promise?" she said thickly.

He stared at her. Hard. "You are one dangerous lady, do you know that?"

"It's not something men tell me often."

"Then they don't know the real you, do they?"

"No," she whispered. "They don't."

"The agency has a strict no-sex rule. You do recall that, don't you?"

"Rules are meant to be broken."

He shook his head at her. "Like I said. Dangerous."

"Dance with me some more."

He laughed. "Not on your life."

"You're supposed to do everything I want you to do tonight."

"Is that so?"

"Yes. It cost me a lot of money for the privilege."

"To be your pretend boyfriend, not your sex slave. It'd cost you a lot more for *that* privilege. Now stop scowling at me and start smiling. I've just spotted her majesty and her faithful lady-in-waiting spying on us from behind those potted palms. If Amber thinks we're fighting, it'll make her night, and we don't want that, do we?"

"I guess not," Josie grumbled and found a smile from somewhere.

But it was a real struggle, her body still burning with a white-hot heat. She wanted Callum so badly she physically ached down there; she also felt so wet it could prove embarrassing to sit down.

"I need to go to the ladies," she muttered through her smiling teeth. "And then I want to go home."

"Oh, no. None of that running away stuff. You came here to show Amber and the rest of your class what a stunning success you are in life, and that's exactly what you're going to do. No way am I going to let you spoil everything now by acting like a typical female."

"In case you haven't noticed I *am* a typical female."

"No, you're not. You're not typical at all. You're quite unique."

"I am?"

"Yes. A bit thick, though."

"I am not thick," she snapped. "I'm very smart."

"In that case use the brains God gave you to realize I'm not rejecting you here. I'm protecting you."

"Protecting me? Against what?"

"Against me, of course. Who else?"

Actually, she'd been thinking of herself.

"Are you that much of a naughty boy with the opposite sex?"

"You'd better believe it, honey. Now, be a sensible girl and off you go to the ladies' room. Meanwhile, I'll go chat to the terrible twosome, find out when supper's on. I'm a mite hungry."

"Be careful what you say to them."

"Trust me."

Trust him? She didn't want to trust him. Neither did she want him protecting her. She wanted him to ravish her. She wanted him to strip away all her clothes and all her inhibitions and take her to all those places she'd never been before but which she'd thought about and dreamt about for so long.

But that isn't going to happen, is it, Josie? Our confessed Casanova is having a crisis of conscience tonight for some weird and wonderful reason and isn't going to come across. Of all the rotten luck!

But that was the way of her luck where men and sex were concerned, wasn't it? She was fated to go to her grave without fulfilling any of her favorite fantasies. Maybe even without being made love to properly once in her whole miserable life!

Really, she would settle for that. One night of good old-fashioned but very good sex. Was that too much to ask? Forget the other adventurous and kinky stuff. No gymnastic positions, or unusual settings. No sexy lingerie or leather corsets or aphrodisiacal oils. Just straightforward foreplay and intercourse. Provided she got to do it more than once, that is. And hopefully had an orgasm or two during the experience.

Josie watched Callum walk away, every gorgeous orgasm-making inch of him. What a waste!

"I'm sure I would have been good in bed with you," she said to herself with a sigh. "But now I guess I'll never know."

Typical!

Squaring her shoulders, Josie headed for the French doors, plastering a smile on her face on the way.

10

SHE WAS SILENT all the way home. Silent and sad-looking.

Callum believed he was doing the right thing by not giving her what she thought she wanted, but still, he felt guilty. Perverse, really. Guilt was supposed to be what you felt when you did the *wrong* thing.

The decision to walk her to her front door was potentially hazardous but how could he dump her outside the house and just drive off? Hardly what a gentleman escort would do. So once again, he did the right thing.

The sight of her front door hanging off its hinges and with a great gaping hole near the dead bolt brought them both to a gasping halt.

"Wait," Callum warned, grabbing Josie's arm when she lurched forward. "My cell phone's in my car. We'll go back there and call the police, then wait till they arrive."

Callum might have forged on inside if it was only his own skin to worry about, but he wasn't going to risk anything happening to Josie.

Already she was pale-faced with shock.

"You think they might still be inside?" she said shakily.

"Probably not. But why take any chances?"

The police came reasonably quickly, considering it was a Saturday night. Apparently, there'd been a spate of such break-ins in the neighborhood; an axe was used to smash down doors, followed by a grab-and-run raid of televisions, DVDs, CD players and computers.

After going through each room, Josie confirmed that was all that was missing, with the final tally being three televisions, a DVD and a video player, her dad's home PC and two portable CD players.

Fortunately, they weren't the type of criminals that vandalized and defaced the properties they robbed, which was something to be grateful for. They also hadn't bothered with the separate studio down at the bottom of the back yard. Josie's mother was a potter of some note and her studio was full of quite valuable ware.

Josie was enormously relieved when she saw everything was intact in there.

"It's a well-organized gang," the police sergeant informed them. "They case out a place and strike with great speed while the occupants are out. They often choose homes like this where the front door is hidden from passersby. They're very slick and they never leave fingerprints. I hate to say this, Ms. Williams, but the chances of your parents getting their property back is remote. I hope they're insured."

"Yes, yes, I'm sure they are."

"You'll need a new door. Possibly some other added security as well. This gang has been known to hit the same place again after enough time has passed for the stolen goods to be replaced."

The sergeant looked straight at Callum who nodded resignedly. "I'll see to everything first thing in the morning."

"You'll stay the night as well, will you, sir? After all, the lady can't lock her front door at the moment."

"Yes. Okay," Callum said. "I'll stay the night."

Josie's eyes snapped up to his at this announcement, her expression more angry than pleased.

"Good," the sergeant said, then turned to Josie. "We'll need a detailed list of what's been stolen, miss. But there's no mad rush. Any time this week will do. Sorry we can't do any more for you tonight but we're working flat out. This is the fourth place we've been called to recently for break-ins of this kind."

After the police left, Callum pushed the front door back onto its hinges as best he could, then jammed the hall stand against it to stop it from falling in again. Josie watched him all the while with that black shawl of hers wrapped defensively around her and her lips pressed tightly together. You could have cut the tension in the air around her with a knife.

"Still protecting me, Callum?" she finally snapped when he finished securing the front door.

He eyed her with a mixture of dry amusement and weary resignation. "No. I've decided I can fight lots of things in life, but not fate."

"You don't have to stay. I am quite capable of looking after myself."

"I've just barricaded us in."

"You can leave by the back door which isn't broken. There's a path up the side of the house."

"I suppose I *could* do that. But I'm not going to."

His conscience wouldn't let him. She didn't realize it yet but shock might set in later, especially if she was alone. Getting robbed was actually quite a traumatic experience. He knew. It had happened to him once, at his house in Glebe. For ages afterward, he'd listened for noises in the night, and slept with a baseball bat under his bed.

He could see her now, lying all alone in her bed later tonight, feeling frightened and insecure.

He wouldn't be able to sleep himself for worrying about her. That was what he'd meant by fate conspiring against him. There was only one thing he could do to solve both their problems. He would sleep in her bed tonight. Neither of them would worry about being robbed if he did that. They'd be too busy doing what they'd both been wanting to do since they'd met.

"I don't want you to stay," she said.

Stupid stubborn woman. "You will."

"What do you mean, I will? I will *when?*" she snapped.

"Very shortly." And with three long-legged strides he covered the distance between them and pulled her into his arms. She struggled in a vain attempt to stop his mouth from capturing hers; struggled and struck out at him, slapping at his shoulders, uncaring when the shawl fell from her shoulders onto the floor.

Callum ignored her ineffectual blows and just held her more tightly, kissing her even more deeply.

She wanted him to make love to her. He knew she did. He just had to get past her silly pride.

When she kept trying to push him away, his mouth

lifted. "What *is* your problem?" he demanded to know, his face hot and his breathing ragged.

"I don't want your pity," she threw at him.

"Pity! You think this is *pity?*" he roared, and picking up her right hand, he placed it firmly over his by now bursting erection.

"Oh," she said, flushing. "Well, I...I...I..."

"I sure like a woman who knows what she wants," he said dryly.

"I *do* know what I want," she countered with a return to the spirit he admired. "You were the one who kept running a mile."

"In case you haven't noticed, I'm not running now. I've decided to surrender and be your sex slave for the night."

"My sex slave?"

"Isn't that what you said you wanted earlier this evening? What you'd paid for? For me to obey your every command?"

"I...I...yes, yes, I suppose I did."

"Then start commanding, mistress. I'm all yours."

"All mine," she said, her voice echoing with wonder and her eyes glittering with excitement.

When they raked possessively up and down his body, a familiar thought started up in Callum's head and he realized why this scenario was suddenly turning him on so much. It reminded him of a long-ago affair. What a truly wicked woman she'd been. Addictive, though.

Callum suspected that Josie might be just as wonderfully wicked, once she got going.

"Just for one night, remember?" he warned, his

voice as thick as treacle. "That's the deal. Take it or leave it."

"I'll take it."

"I thought you might."

"Kiss me again," she ordered huskily. "And don't stop till I tell you to."

Don't stop what? Callum wondered as his lips covered hers. But then she moaned under his mouth and he decided it didn't matter, because nothing was going to stop him now. She thought she was going to be the boss in the bedroom tonight, but that was because he was happy to let her think that. The days of Callum being any woman's plaything were long gone. Still, erotic games could be fun and the thought of playing sex slave to Josie's dominatrix just for tonight was tantalizingly tempting.

Callum's conscience was soothed by the fact that that kind of fantasy role-playing didn't lend itself to emotional involvement, because he and Josie wouldn't be making love as such. They'd just be having sex. She might want more of the same in the morning, but not because she thought she'd fallen for him. It would be more climaxes she'd be looking for, not love.

She could find that with a whole host of men, not just him.

Now why did that thought rankle so much?

The male ego was a perverse creature, Callum decided. He didn't want Josie to care about him, but at the same time, he didn't want her not to.

Her mouth wrenched away from his and she stared up at him, eyes wide and face flushed.

"You do realize I don't do usually do this sort of thing," she said breathlessly.

"What sort of thing?"

"Go to bed with a man on the first date."

"I'm not a real date, though, am I? I'm a paid escort. Which you were at great pains to remind me already a few times tonight."

His statement seemed to bother her, for some reason. "Yes, but that doesn't mean that I don't genuinely like you."

"Or I you. You can't pay for an erection any more than you can get one through pity. Look, you don't need to do this, Josie."

"Do what?"

"Play some kind of good-girl game. I already believe you're a good girl. I also believe good girls enjoy sex for sex's sake as much as so-called bad girls. So you don't have to justify yourself to me. I'm with you all the way in this regard. But I can't stand girls who pretend, especially to themselves. Admit that having me stay the night was what you had in mind all evening, then just go for it."

"Go for it," she repeated dazedly.

"Yes. Tell me what you want me to do."

"What I want you to do…"

Callum soon realized that if he waited for Josie to decide what she wanted to do next, they'd be standing in the hallway staring at each other all night.

"Let's start at the beginning again," he suggested, and bent to kiss her once more.

This time, he kissed her more slowly, taking his time to sensitize her lips first, tugging at them with his teeth, then sucking each one in turn between his own lips before finally moving his tongue into her mouth. But not deeply, or aggressively. He let it slide gently in and out, then up and around, touching his tongue tip to her palate, the insides of her cheeks, the underside of her tongue. If the way she moaned and clung to his shoulders was any guide, she liked that kind of slow kissing a lot.

Callum loved hearing the sounds of her pleasure. Without stopping the kissing his hands found the hidden hook and eye at the nape of her neck and moved them apart. Once the halter straps were released, he eased the dress down over the hurdle of her hardtipped breasts, after which he let it slip from his fingers to slither down her body into a pool at her feet. Only then did she seem to notice what he'd been doing, her mouth gasping away from his.

"You told me not to stop kissing you," he reminded her, and pulled her back against him, capturing her mouth again in a far more hungry kiss. That short glimpse of her perfect breasts with their fiercely erect nipples had done surprising things to his control, making him impatient with slow kissing. She was on fire as well, her hips moving restlessly against him in a silent but agitated plea for more.

Callum decided enough was enough. She wanted him. He wanted her. They didn't need endless foreplay. Not the first time, anyway.

She whimpered when he abruptly stopped the kissing, then gaped when he swept her up off the floor into his arms.

"Which way to your bedroom?" he asked, startled to find that his own voice was not too steady.

"No," she said, and he glowered down into her eyes.

"Don't start that nonsense again."

"No, I mean no, I don't want to go to *my* bedroom. It only has a single bed in it. We'll go the main guest room. It has a really big bed in it."

"Good thinking," he said. If he recalled rightly, what she was referring to was more of a suite than a room, with a separate sitting area and en suite bathroom. "Up these steps, wasn't it?" And he headed straight for the small staircase on the right. The steps on the left led down to the living areas, he remembered, with the master bedroom and two other bedrooms farther down on an even lower level.

Callum had followed in Josie's wake earlier when she'd gone through the house, turning on all the lights and checking to see what had been stolen. With his good memory for floor plans and excellent sense of direction, he pretty well already knew where everything was. The guest suite—which looked like a recent addition—was located over the garages.

"Our own private orgy palace," Callum said as he carried her in, bypassing the cosy sitting room in favor of the bedroom. "You were right. Great bed," he complimented as he threw back the bedclothes and stretched her out on the crisp clean sheets.

That done, he sat and took off her shoes, tossing them into a corner. All that remained now between Josie and total nudity was her black satin G-string.

Was that fear in her eyes? Surely not. What was there to be afraid of?

Maybe she was worried about how she looked in the nude, like some women were. That was why they preferred dim lights, and sometimes total darkness. Not wanting anything to spoil things for her, Callum reached to switch on one of the bedside lamps, then walked over to turn off the ceiling light. When he returned to the bed, he bent to give her another hungry kiss before hooking his fingers over the waistband of her panties and gently peeling them down her legs and off her feet.

His stomach crunched down hard at the sight of that triangle of dark curls, more blood rushing to his already aching erection. How odd, he thought, that the removal of that ineffectual scrap of satin could be so arousing. Hell, he had to get his own clothes off before he lost it. And he had to stop staring at her down there.

"Callum," she said in a taut little voice.

"Hush," he said as he threw aside his jacket and began reefing off his bow tie. "No need for you to worry or do anything. Just lie back and enjoy."

That, she did, if the avid gleam in her gaze was anything to go by. She fairly gobbled him up as he stripped down to his waist, the sight of his bared chest seeming to find favor.

Callum's body was the one area where he surpassed his kid brother in sex appeal. He was built, in every area. He didn't have to work out in gyms to maintain his broad-shouldered frame. The structure and the size were God-given assets, although his active lifestyle kept him fit. Still, it was good not having to ever feel shy or inhibited about taking off his clothes.

Callum reached into his trousers to empty the pocket before taking them off when he remembered he didn't even have a single condom on him.

"Damn!" he swore as he tipped his keys and wallet onto the bedside table.

She sat bolt upright on the bed, eyes alarmed. "What?"

"I don't have any condoms on me. I didn't realize I might need some tonight. Do you have any?"

"In my bedside drawer," she confessed. "There's… um…a new box."

"Great. I'll go get it. The bedroom with the single bed in it, right?"

"Right."

"Won't be long."

He wasn't, retrieving the unopened box from where she'd said it would be—the ribbed and well-lubricated kind, he noted—and hurrying straight back.

Finding the bedroom empty on his return startled him, till he noticed the closed bathroom door. Sighing, he ripped open the box of condoms, poured a few out onto the bedside chest, then slipped the rest in the top drawer. He was about to take off his trousers when the sound of taps being turned on sent him rushing to rap hard on the door.

"What are you doing in there?" he called out.

"I…I thought I should have a shower."

"No! No. Don't do that." Why did women think they had to do that all the time, jump into the shower and wash, as though they were dirty, or something. A girl like Josie would have showered or bathed before she went out tonight, as did he. Callum adored the musky scent of a turned-on woman. The smell of soap did nothing for him at all.

"Open this door, Josie," he said firmly.

She opened the door, blinking up at him with those gorgeous dark eyes of hers. "Why can't I have a shower?" she asked, her voice trembling, a cream towel clutched around her body.

"Because I don't want you washed and dried," he said, reaching out to take the towel from her trembling fingers, leaving her standing naked before him and looking even more beautiful than when she'd been on the bed, if that were possible.

Callum felt his flesh leap, then begin to swell further, which was a miracle, considering he already had a hard-on the size of the Centrepoint Tower.

Hell, but he couldn't wait to sink himself into the hot wet depths of her exquisitely feminine body, to wind his hands into that glorious curtain of black hair, to pull her head back and watch her mouth gasp wide.

Callum was no stranger to the urgings of lust, but he couldn't remember ever feeling quite so driven, or impatient. Normally, with a woman, he took his time, enjoying long hours of foreplay before moving on to straight sex. Right now, it took all of his control not to ram her up against the bathroom wall and do it to her right then and there.

"I want you wet," he ground out, tossing aside the towel and scooping her naked body up into his arms. "And I want you *now!*"

11

HE WANTED HER NOW!

Josie had never known such passion. Or such impatience.

Yet oh…it was so exciting.

He dumped her quite roughly back across the bed before standing wide-legged at her feet, his blue eyes glittering wildly as his hands went to the waistband of his pants.

If his stripping down to his waist had titillated her earlier, his ripping off the rest of his clothes turned Josie on to the max. Her heart began going like a jackhammer behind her ribs, her nipples standing to attention like twin tin soldiers. When Callum finally stood stark naked before her, her mouth dropped inelegantly open.

"If you keep looking at me like that," he warned as he reached for a condom, "I won't win the first time award." And he ripped the foil packet open with his teeth. "But not to worry," he went on as he protected them both with amazing speed. "Regardless of the outcome, I'll do better the second time round, infinitely better by the third and bloody brilliant on the fourth."

Josie just stared at him. At his eyes, this time.

Surely he was joking. No man could do it that many times. Not in one night. Not a real man.

Her fantasy man could, of course. But that was fiction and this was... Her eyes dropped again to what had to be the most impressive erection she'd ever seen. Nothing fictional about that, she conceded, her insides squeezing tight in anticipation of how it would feel, sliding into her.

She'd struck the jackpot at long last!

"I thought I told you to stop looking at me like that," he muttered, shocking her when he took her ankles and pulled her by the legs till her bottom was resting on the edge of the bed. She had no time to protest—not that she wanted to—before a pillow was stuffed under her hips, her legs were pried apart and he was there, between her thighs, his flesh already filling hers.

Oh my, she thought dazedly. Oh my my *my!*

When she made a whimpering sound, he withdrew a little, which was the last thing she wanted.

He muttered something unintelligible before picking up her legs and hooking her ankles over his shoulders like she'd read about in that magazine article. Despite this lifting her bottom right off the pillow, leaving only her upper half on the bed, it was a surprisingly comfortable position, especially once he cradled her buttocks in his hands.

"That feel better?"

"It felt all right before," she managed to answer in a highly breathless fashion. Heavens to Betsy, if her heart went any faster she would explode.

His eyes carried some confusion. "But I thought...I

mean…Oh, never mind. This'll be better for you, anyway. It'll hit your G-spot.''

Her G-spot! He knew where it was, even if she didn't.

His hands kneaded her bottom as he started to move inside her, rocking back and forth with short sharp jabs. Josie wasn't sure if he'd found her G-spot straightaway but she certainly started feeling sensations she'd never felt before during sex, a pressure. On each downward stroke, the pressure built and built. She could think of nothing else but that part of her, her body tensing in anticipation of each forward thrust of his flesh.

Was it blissful pleasure she was experiencing? Not really. Yet for all that, the feelings he was producing were addictive and compelling. If he'd stopped, she would have cried out in dismay. No, not dismay. Despair. He had to go on. *Had* to.

Her moans might have been embarrassing if her brain had been capable of anything but focusing on just that thought; that he not stop what he was doing.

His face was a taut grimace, telling her of his own tension. She had to admire his control. Already, most men she'd been to bed with would have come, and gone. She still hadn't come yet herself but she knew she was going to. Soon…Soon…

Her insides contracted with her rapidly escalating need for release, her head thrashing from side to side.

Callum muttered, then changed position again, taking her legs off his shoulders and wrapping them around his waist. Her bottom sagged back onto the pillow. His hands gripped her hips and his thrusting, when it returned, was powerful and deep.

Josie instinctively squeezed his flesh with her own, her back arching in frantic tandem with his movements. "Don't stop," she panted. "Please don't stop."

"God," he groaned. "I can't hang on much longer. I just can't…I'm sorry, sweetheart, I…"

Her cry of sudden and rapturous release interrupted his desperate warnings, her first fierce spasm catapulting him over the edge with her.

His roar totally drowned out her own naked cry.

Not in her wildest dreams, had Josie imagined such an incredible experience. In one split second, all that pent-up pressure splintered apart as wave after wave of pure pleasure engulfed her. All she'd ever read about the joys of sex finally made sense to her. Not fiction at all, she realized, once the man was right. Not fantasy, but fact. Not a dream, but reality; brilliant, mind-blowing reality!

Her flesh kept shuddering with delight, as did his, the obvious intensity of his climax heightening her satisfaction. She wished it would never end, but of course it did, the spasms slowing, then finally stopping altogether. With a perverse feeling of disappointment, her fists uncurled, her wrists went limp and her legs started to lose their grip on his waist.

Callum's grabbing her hands and pulling her upright startled her.

"Hold on," he said, and scooped her right up off the bed. She clung to him like a monkey, her hands snaked up around his neck, her legs tightening again around his waist. Their flesh was still fused as one and his, amazingly, didn't feel all that soft, or all that small. Suddenly, any looming lethargy was banished from her body, all her sensitive nerve-endings on alert once more.

"Where…where are we going?" she asked when he started to walk around the foot of the bed, the to and fro movement caused by his long strides sending electric sparks all through her. If he kept walking, she would come again.

"I thought we might have that shower you wanted earlier."

"Together?" she choked out.

"Sure. Why not."

Josie swallowed, not able to find words to express her surprise. When she'd been married to Peter, they *never* shared the shower, or even the bathroom.

Yet Callum obviously considered the idea not only acceptable, but normal.

As much as Josie found his attitude startling, she also thought it quite wonderful. At last, a man who actually liked his own body, as well as hers. A man who wasn't constrained by never-ending inhibitions and overly prudish ways.

"Look, I know I said I didn't want you showering earlier," Callum continued as he carried her into the bathroom, cupping her bottom with one large hand while he turned on the shower taps with the other. "That's another reason why I'm getting into this shower with you. To stop you from going mad, washing yourself all over too much. But you can wash me all over as much as you like," he added with a wicked but wry grin. "I know you girls. Most of you like a guy to be as fresh as a daisy before you'd dream of going down on him. Okay?"

"Okay," she said with a succinct simplicity which did not reflect the mad rush of excitement racing through her veins. The thought of washing him all over down there, and then actually going down on him was the stuff her dreams were made of.

Maybe she *was* a pervert like Peter had said. But she didn't think so. No, she didn't think so at all. *He'd* been the weird one. He'd never let her do that no matter how often she'd tried. As for his going down on her... Forget it! He'd said that kind of thing was for filthy animals, not decent human beings.

As for the other men she'd been with since her marriage...

Well...as she'd decided earlier, she hadn't really given them a fair go. She'd automatically shied away from oral sex, for starters, unable to get over the feelings of self-disgust Peter had brainwashed into her.

So where were those feelings tonight?

Gone, she realized. True, she was still slightly nervous over some of the things Callum was suggesting. But not disgusted, or repulsed. She actually found his ways a real turn-on. What else would he want to do to her tonight? And her to him?

Everything, she hoped.

Josie was ripe and ready for everything. She was ripe and ready for a night when all her fantasies were enacted out for real. In short, she was ripe and ready for a lover like Callum McCloud.

JOSIE WOKE FIRST, uncurling from the fetal position she liked to sleep in and gradually becoming aware that this wasn't her bed. Or her room.

When her brain finally clicked into gear she sucked in sharply, then peeked under the sheet which had been pulled up to her neck. Since she always slept in a nightgown, the sight of her very naked body confirmed what Josie already suspected; that her memories of the night before hadn't been some over-the-top dream. It had been very real! The fact she was in the guest bedroom also indicated that her wild erotic romp with her gentleman escort had certainly been fact, not fantasy. On top of that, she could hear breathing. Deep, even breathing. Close by. *Very* close by.

Holding her own breath, she rolled over to see the evidence of her first one-night stand at first hand.

And there he was, as large as life. Larger, actually, in the cold light of morning. And just as naked as she was. But in his case, the sheet wasn't covering all that much of him. Only his legs. Thank goodness he was face down, she thought, even as her gaze gobbled up what was on view. What a gorgeous back he had! And what arms. His tight buns were a sight for sore eyes as well, though the red nail marks raked across them brought color to her face.

She'd done that.

There again, what *hadn't* she done?

Josie smiled a naughty and highly self-satisfied smile. She'd been good in bed with him, just as she'd thought she would be. As for Callum, she was going to dub him the eighth wonder of the world!

What that man didn't know about a woman's body

wasn't worth knowing. Unerringly, he knew exactly what to do to turn her on again, even when she thought she couldn't possibly have another climax. During their torrid hours of lovemaking, she'd experienced most of those positions listed in that magazine, as well as all the things a woman liked a man to do to them in bed. And then some.

She shuddered when she thought of how she'd surrendered her entire body to him. But it was not a shudder of shock or disgust. More a reliving of remembered ecstasy. Her body had shuddered under Callum's so many times she'd lost count. He was the fantasy man she'd always craved. Her dream lover.

And he was still there, beside her. He hadn't snuck away in the middle of the night, or been up and dressed first thing this morning, eager to say a hurried goodbye.

A sudden frown creased Josie's forehead. Was that because he'd promised the police he would stay, or because he wanted more of the same?

Surely he couldn't just get up and walk away from what they'd shared last night. Surely, he would want more, just as she wanted more. Admittedly, Callum had warned her that she could only expect the one night from him. But had he really meant it? Or was that just a male ploy to give himself an excuse for a quick exit in the morning if the girl didn't come up to scratch, sex-wise?

Josie had no idea. She wasn't exactly experienced at one-night stands. As much as she thought she'd been pretty good in bed, perhaps she'd just been so-so. She hardly had a yardstick to measure her performance by. Maybe Callum was used to far more sophisticated and aggressive women. Josie conceded she had been more the recipient last night, rather than the giver. True, she'd been on top once, but only with his encouragement.

Josie gnawed at her bottom lip as she tried to remember if she'd ever actually taken the assertive role. Mmmm. She *had* gone down on him. *Twice*. But at his urging, not off her own bat. And she hadn't gone all the way on either occasion. He'd stopped her before she could. Which she had to confess she'd been happy with at the time. Bad mental programming was not totally dispensed of in one night, she'd discovered. Her flesh had been willing but her mind had still been a bit weak. But she'd sure like the chance to try again. And she wanted to try with Callum!

If he'd been lying on his back, she could have started trying right now, while he was still asleep. She imagined a man wouldn't mind waking to the feel of tender fingers on his private parts. Not to mention a warm wet mouth. She knew she'd have loved it, if she were a man. She'd loved Callum's mouth on her last night. And how!

As though she'd conveyed the idea to his subconscious, Callum made a softly sighing sound then rolled over onto his back. But his eyes remained firmly shut.

Josie stared down at his slumbering penis—still a formidable size at rest—her mouth drying at the thought of bending her head and licking its velvety tip till it woke from its slumber. Till *he* woke.

Her sigh was full of regret, because as much as she wanted to, she just couldn't bring herself to do it. She simply didn't have that kind of boldness yet. The truth was she didn't even know what she was going to do or say when Callum finally woke up. This was hardly a scenario she was familiar with.

She needed advice and she needed it fast.

A glance at the bedside clock radio showed it was quite late. Nine-twenty. Kay would have been up for hours. Her daughter, little Katie, was an early riser.

Kay would know what she should do. Kay was always a fount of information where men and sex were concerned. She wouldn't be too shocked, either, like Lisa and Deb might be. Heck, they thought she was frigid! Besides, what advice could they give her? Their relationships were always disasters, like hers.

Yes, she would call Kay, confess all, then ask how she should act this morning to convince Callum she didn't want commitment from him, just some more mind-blowing sex. She understood that a guy as young and restless as he was, wasn't interested in having a steady girlfriend. Besides, hadn't he said he was off overseas again soon?

As much as Josie would rather he stay in Sydney indefinitely—it would be hard to have sex with a guy who wasn't in the darned country—Josie was a realist. There was no real future for her with the likes of Callum McCloud. There was, however, a wealth of experience to be gained from him, even on a short-term basis. What she wanted to propose was a strictly sexual affair till he took off. Was that too much to ask?

No, Josie decided. Definitely not. Most young guys would jump at the chance.

Of course, such proposals had to be worded carefully lest the male in question thought you were trying to trap him into a relationship. Which was why she needed Kay's advice. This was a sticky situation.

Swinging her feet over the side of the bed onto the pale peach carpet, Josie levered herself upright and tiptoed from the room, scooping up her clothes as she went. Hurrying down to her bedroom she threw her things onto the bed then drew on her pale blue wrap before dashing back up to the kitchen, and the phone.

Kay didn't answer till the sixth ring, some butterflies gathering in Josie's stomach in the meanwhile. As much as she knew Kay wouldn't be too shocked, it was still going to be difficult confessing to her bold behavior.

"Kay, it's me, Josie. Have I called at a bad time?"

"No, not at all, Colin's taken Katie to the park and I was doing some laundry. Actually, I'm *so* glad you phoned," Kay swept on before Josie could open her mouth. "I've been wanting to talk to you since I got up this morning, but didn't think you'd appreciate a call at six. I've been dying to know how it went last night. Please don't tell me you're calling to confess that you went to bed with Beau Grainger last night and that he's still there."

"What?" Josie said, taken aback that Kay had jumped to the right conclusion. After all, it wasn't a likely scenario, given that the escort agency had a strict no-sex rule and she herself was not known for coming on to men on a first date. "Why on earth would you think that?"

"Oh, thank goodness. Obviously, you didn't. But I was really worried, I can tell you. Gigolos like that know all the right moves to get a girl into bed. Still, he probably only targets his older women clients.''

Gigolo? Why was Kay suddenly calling Callum a gigolo? *She* was the one who'd recommended him. Her cousin had said he was exactly what that agency supplied, a gentleman escort.

''I'm not sure I'm following you, Kay.''

''No. Sorry. I'm getting way ahead of myself. The thing is we had this family get-together last night and who should be there but Cora. Well, we got to gossiping and I told her you'd hired Beau Grainger to take you to your class reunion. I didn't think you'd mind her knowing since your paths never cross. Anyway, when she looked so darned worried at this news, I asked what was up and she told me the truth this time.''

''The...truth?'' Josie echoed, a new and more vigorous swarm of butterflies fluttering in her stomach.

''Yes. Apparently, our so-called gentleman escort seduced Cora when they got home, taking full advantage of the fact she was drunk. *And* he stayed the whole night. She agreed he was incredible in the sack and she'd never known sex like it. The trouble was the next morning he brought up the subject of payment for services rendered. An embarrassed Cora pretended she'd always known she had to pay him extra for the sex and coughed up three hundred dollars. She admitted to me she wasn't actually all that upset about the incident. She said he was well worth the money and she was tempted to hire him again. But she wasn't sure if someone like you could cope if confronted with the same situation. Still, he didn't seduce you so there's no problem, is there? Maybe he doesn't dare pull that trick too often. Or as I said earlier, he only targets the type of women who won't call the agency and complain. But enough of that, did he do a good job as a pretend boyfriend or not? And how did the reunion go? Tell me all.''

Josie's thoughts were whirling by this point, various things Callum had said the night before now making sense, especially his reminding her in the hallway that she knew what she wanted from him when she hired him and to just go for it. Obviously, he thought she'd been aware of his reputation as a paid stud all along! And had hired him anyway.

Now she knew how Callum had worked his way around the world. By selling himself to women.

The disillusionment Kay had spoken about was quick to rear its worrying head, but this time, Josie dismissed it quite ruthlessly. So Callum probably expected to be paid extra for his sexual services. So what? He still had to have found her reasonably desirable to perform so often and so well.

Josie was determined not to overreact to Kay's news, or to start falling apart again. That kind of wishy-washy behavior was not in keeping with her new, bold, sexually liberated self.

Which I have Callum to thank for, might I add!

So he was an amateur gigolo. Good. That solved her problem. If his body was for hire, then she'd simply hire it again. And again. And again. Till she'd experienced everything in that magazine.

The thought excited Josie more than she could

ever imagine. This was real liberation, she reasoned elatedly.

But she couldn't tell Kay her plans. As unshockable as her friend and colleague claimed to be about men and sex, Josie felt sure she would balk at the idea of Josie paying this fellow to fulfil all her fantasies. Josie decided to tell Kay exactly what she wanted to hear. That Callum—alias the infamous Beau Grainger—had been the perfect pretend boyfriend; that Amber had had her nose put right out of joint; and that the night had given Josie nothing but pure pleasure and great satisfaction.

She smiled at this last little pun. Truly, she'd turned into a right devil overnight!

She would not mention the robbery, lest she slip up over relating events after Callum brought her home. She would not even mention Callum's real name. She would stick to the Beau Grainger alias.

"So you want me to tell you all," Josie said brightly as she picked up the kettle and starting filling it under the tap. "Now that's a tall order." Very tall, if she'd been going to tell the truth. The sanitized version was going to be much much shorter. "Let's see now…"

12

CALLUM STIRRED from sleep to the smell of coffee.

Lifting one eyelid, he was startled to see a smiling Josie standing by the bed, a breakfast tray in her hands. His other eye shot open and he pulled himself up into a sitting position, whipping the sheet more modestly up around his waist, then patting his lap.

"Now this is what I call service," he said with a grin, having already decided during the night not to have any regrets this morning.

Frankly, he hadn't been with such an exciting sexual partner in a very long time. Josie clearly liked to be dominated by her man. Her willingness to do whatever *he* wanted to do had brought out the beast in him all right. He'd really gone to town in this bed last night and he'd loved every moment. How could you ever regret sex as great as that?

"I hope you like toasted bagels," she said.

"Love 'em."

"I know the coffee is exactly as you like it. Black and strong. I remembered from supper last night."

"Aah. That fantastic memory of yours still working well, I see."

"What? Oh yes…my fantastic memory. You have a pretty good one yourself."

"Careful," he warned when she started lowering the tray across his thighs. The steaming coffee mug was full to the brim and it wouldn't take much for it to spill.

She smiled a saucy little smile and his flesh twitched in response. Man, but she was the sexiest girl.

"Would I dream of damaging that very impressive equipment of yours?" she quipped, and he laughed.

"You're very bright-eyed and bushy-tailed this morning," he said, steadying the tray and looking her up and down at the same time.

She was wearing a short silky blue robe and nothing else, if he was any judge. She had not a scrap of makeup on and her gorgeous black hair was up in a high ponytail. She looked considerably younger than her twenty-eight years. Only in her eyes could he see the passionate and very adult woman who last night had complemented his own rather primal male desires.

"Amazing what a dozen orgasms will do for a woman," came her sassy remark.

"Only a dozen?"

"Arrogant devil."

He grinned, then picked up the mug of coffee and locked eyes with her over the rim.

"Blue suits you," he said after a couple of sips.

"Thank you. And brown suits you."

"Brown?"

"Your birthday suit is brown," she said with a nod toward his bare chest.

He laughed again. Not only beautiful but brainy, and yes, bold. But a different kind of bold from his usual bed-mate. Josie knew when to be assertive and sassy, and when to be all soft surrender. He simply wasn't going to be able to keep to his other decision to leave this at one night. He wanted more of Josie than that. At the same time, he didn't want to make promises he wasn't going to keep. It was going to be tricky having his cake and eating it too. He wondered if she'd agree to just having a fling with him till he left for San Francisco?

Callum was puzzling over how to broach the subject when he noticed a piece of paper sticking out from under the plate which held the bagels.

"What's this?" he asked, tugging it out with his free hand and staring down at a blank check. His head jerked back when he saw it was made out to him. What was going on here?

"I didn't fill in the amount," she said as she perched on the side of the bed, "because I didn't know how much you would charge me."

"For what?"

"For last night."

"Oh. Yes. Last night. But you…er…pre-paid the agency, didn't you?"

"Not *that* part of last night, silly," she said, and a telling color crept into her cheeks.

Her meaning only took a split second to sink in, and Callum couldn't have been more taken aback. Till he recalled that he'd been standing in for Clay last night. What had that boy been up to?

"Look, let's not play games here, Callum," Josie went on before he could find his tongue. "I know you go to bed with your clients for money, if they're willing. And goodness knows I was willing enough last night. Fact is if you're not too expensive, I'd like to hire you again.''

Callum could only stare at her as his feelings swung from anger at Clay to shock at Josie for actually hiring an escort, *believing* he was a stud for hire. And now, being prepared to hire him again!

At the same time, Callum couldn't help feeling perversely flattered. And seriously tempted. To let Josie hire him again was certainly a way to have more sex with her without strings. It was actually a titillating scenario, being paid for your sexual services.

But he still couldn't bring himself to do it. How could he preach honesty with women to his kid brother—as well as tear strips off Clay for virtually prostituting himself—if *he* turned around and did the same thing himself?

Women hated being deceived. Which reminded him. He'd already deceived Josie on a fairly large scale last night, although his intentions had been good. Sort of. To begin with.

Josie wasn't going to be too happy when he told her the truth.

''For heaven's sake, Callum,'' Josie said, ''why are you looking at me like that?''

Callum gathered himself, and his thoughts. It might be a good idea if he found some more facts about Clay's past behavior before he launched into his confession. ''I'm curious over why you would think my body was for hire. I mean, considering *Gentlemen Partners* has a strict no-sex policy between escort and client.''

Now it was Josie looking confused. ''Are you saying that I got it wrong? Look, Callum, maybe you don't make a habit of it, but I *know* you charged at least one woman for sex. The lady who recommended you to me told Kay all about it. Three hundred dollars it cost her for the night she spent with you. Not that she's complaining. She said you were well worth every cent.''

Callum winced. Oh Clay, you foolish, foolish boy. If you needed money that badly why didn't you just call me?

Callum put down the coffee mug, took the check in both hands and started ripping it up.

''What…what are you doing that for?'' Josie said, clearly startled.

''Let's just say you did get it wrong. I *don't* charge women for sex. Obviously, however, my brother did.''

''Huh?''

''This may come as a shock to you, Josie, but you didn't hire me last night. You actually hired my younger brother, Clay. He's the actor in the family. And the fool.''

''I…I don't understand.''

''Then let me explain. Clay's been working for *Gentlemen Partners* to make ends meet while he's been trying to make it as an actor. Anyway, he desperately wanted to go to some party last night to meet a couple of Hollywood big boys out here in Sydney looking for a new Aussie male star. But he was already committed to taking you to your reunion. He begged me to stand in for him. He insisted I pretend to be him so that there'd be no trouble at the agency, which is why I started out last night using that stupid name, but in the end I just couldn't hack it. Hence the return to my real name.''

"So you're not and never have been Beau Grainger?" she asked a bit dazedly.

"No. That's Clay's escort pseudonym. During my role as your pretend boyfriend I told the absolute truth to you and your classmates, because I'm no actor. I am exactly what I said I was. An engineer who works overseas and comes home to Sydney every now and then to visit my brother and check that my house is still in one piece. I flew in yesterday morning from Hawaii after a three-month stint there and I leave for the States in ten days' time.''

Did she look disappointed or distressed with his news? No. Not really. Just startled. But it was important for Callum to keep watching her reactions. Of all the women he'd had ever met, Josie was the one he would most hate to hurt. He liked her enormously and wanted nothing but good things for her. He was yet to gauge if having a brief fling with him would be good for her, though the evidence so far was on the plus side. Any girl who was prepared to pay for sex had to be looking for strictly sexual solace, and not emotional involvement.

"I *am* thirty years old by the way,'' he went on, "Clay's the one who's twenty-four. I'm single and might I add I aim to stay that way. Most important of all, however, is the fact I *don't* go to bed with women for money. I go to bed with them because I want to. I need to be with a woman who turns me on. You turned me on last night, Josie. One hell of a lot.''

A stunned Josie stood up and made her way around

to the foot of the bed, not sure if she was delighted or disappointed. One part of her was thrilled that Callum had taken her bed because he'd wanted to. There'd been something dismaying about thinking he was a gigolo. But the part of her who'd been eagerly going to hire him again now worried that she was never going to spend another night with him. Callum obviously kept his sex life to one-night stands. You didn't have to be a genius to read between the lines.

"Say something," he said brusquely.

"I...I don't know what to say."

"Tell me you're not angry with me."

"What? No! No, why should I be? You were wonderful last night."

"Funny. You don't look too pleased."

"I'm disappointed that I can't hire you again."

His glance was sharp, his eyes oddly relieved.

"You don't have to be," he said. "You can have all you want of me for free."

"What?" Josie's head whirled.

"Till I head back overseas, that is," he added, dashing any hope that he might want to date her, with a view to something more lasting and meaningful. "I leave a week from Tuesday, so I'm all yours for the next nine days and nine nights."

The thought of nine more nights like last night sent Josie's head spinning further and her blood fizzing along her veins. When her knees went to water she reached out to grip the wrought-iron bed end with both hands.

"But then that's it?" she said, sounding amazingly cool and deliberate, yet inside she was quaking. Still, it was important to Josie to know up front there was no hope of a real relationship. That way, she wouldn't start hoping for one, like she always did.

"Yep. That's it. I have to be honest with you, Josie. I do have the occasional longer relationship with a woman, but only when I'm located in one place for a few months. They never last. When I move on, I move on. I know that sounds like I'm some kind of callous womanizer, but I'm not. The ladies I date always know the score because I tell them, just like I'm telling you. Trust me when I say that a week from Tuesday, I'm outta Sydney and outta your life. I decided a long time ago that marriage and family were not for me. I won't live with a woman either, because when you do that, they soon start imagining that a forever commitment is on the horizon. I'm just not and never will be a forever kind of guy. I am, however, a normal healthy heterosexual male and I like sex, especially the kind of sex I had with you last night. You are one exciting woman."

"I am?" she echoed, thinking more excited than exciting.

"Don't sound so shocked. You must know you're incredibly sexy. Not many women can come that many times in one night."

"Can't they?" Josie stared at him and thought she might come just *thinking* about being with him again.

"Is that why you hired me?" he asked, then smiled a dry smile. "I mean…why you hired a man you thought was a professional stud. Was that because most men haven't satisfied you the way you want to be satisfied?"

Josie almost laughed, that was so funny. But she didn't. She maintained her decorum. It seemed imperative that she at least show a semblance of control here or Callum might think he'd come across some crazy nymphomaniac. She didn't want to say or do anything to make him retract his incredibly exciting proposal. At the same time, she didn't want to pretend to be something she wasn't. She wanted to be as honest with him as he'd been with her. Which meant she had to explain that she wasn't some super-sexed, incredibly brazen creature who'd gone out and hired some gigolo for the night, made mad passionate love with him for hours on end, then waltzed up the next morning with a blank check on the breakfast tray, saying she wanted to hire him again.

Little did he know but when she'd walked in here a short time ago, she'd been quivering in her skin. Her whole woman-of-the-world facade had been…a facade.

"I…uh…have a confession of my own to make," she said, and Callum immediately looked wary.

"Oh? What?"

"I had no idea about your…about Beau Grainger's reputation as a stud for hire when I hired him. It was more his acting ability that appealed, plus the fact he was reputedly so good-looking. I wanted to show up at my class reunion with a handsome hunk on my arm."

"I see… Is that why you looked so surprised when I turned up? Because I wasn't as good-looking at you thought I'd be?"

"Are you crazy? When you showed up, I thought

all my Christmases had come at once. You were just so perfect for the part I had in mind. But that part didn't include sex, Callum. Not at first, although I liked you right away. It wasn't till I thought you liked me back that I started wanting more from you than just a pretend lover. When I went to bed with you last night I knew nothing about Beau Grainger's taking money for sex ever before. I didn't find that out till this morning when I called Kay to tell her what a fantastic night I had with you. Before I could say a word, she told me that her cousin had confessed just last night to having to pay you—I mean your brother—for his sexual services.''

"So what did you tell Kay about me then?''

"Not a word. I let her think you did your job at the reunion like a real trouper and then went home like a gentleman escort would. I didn't even tell her about the robbery in case she started asking me detailed questions and I slipped up. I'd already decided to hire you again.''

"So now we're back to my original question. Why did you want to hire me again? I mean, a girl as gorgeous and sexy as you could get as much free sex as you want.''

Josie's stomach churned at the thought of telling him what a failure her sex life had been up till now. But really, she had no option. "My reason was exactly the reason you guessed,'' she said with a sigh. "No man till you has ever satisfied me. Not even remotely.''

"I find that hard to believe. You're an incredibly

responsive woman. A delight in bed. And marvelously uninhibited.''

Josie finally let go the bed-end to come round and sit on the side of the bed. "Some men don't like uninhibited. My husband sure didn't. He called me a nymphomaniac.''

"You're joking.''

"Not at all. I've never done a lot of the things I did with you before last night.''

"This is unbelievable. I would have thought a girl like yourself would have had lots of experience.''

"I wish. Would you like a brief rundown on my sexual experiences to date?''

"I'm all ears.''

So she told him. And he listened, bless him, with sympathy and real understanding, eating his bagels and drinking his coffee while she told her sorry tale.

"But that's appalling, Josie!'' he exclaimed when she'd finished. "Thank goodness I came along when I did or you might never have known how great you are in bed. And I mean that. You obviously have an instinct for sex which can't be taught. You are a naturally born sensualist.''

Josie was thrilled by his comments, and his wonderfully down-to-earth attitude. It made her feel free to confide things to him which she had never told another human being.

"I've always been interested in sex,'' she admitted. "When I was younger, I tried to keep my interest hidden because I thought nice girls shouldn't be so... well...fascinated by the subject. I waited till I left school to lose my virginity because I didn't want boys thinking I was promiscuous. It was a serious shock to me when my first experience was so bad.''

''A lot of first experiences for girls are bad, if their partner is inept, which yours obviously was.''

''I'll bet you were never inept,'' she said.

He laughed. ''Don't you believe it. There was a time when I was hopeless at sex.''

''Well you're not now.''

''I sincerely hope not. I've had enough practice.''

Josie didn't doubt it. He'd probably had affairs with women in every major city of the world. Exciting experienced exotic women. If she'd been good in bed with him last night, she had him to thank for that. He'd done the leading and she'd just followed.

''You fulfilled most of my sexual wish list last night, do you know that?'' she told him.

''Only most?'' he teased. ''What did I leave out?''

''What? Oh, nothing much, really.''

''Don't go all coy on me, Josie. You were being bluntly honest with me before. I appreciate honesty, especially from the women I date. Believe me when I say I wouldn't entertain the thought of spending more time with you if you weren't the sort of girl who feels comfortable with the idea of enjoying sex for sex's sake, which you obviously do. Now, don't look a gift horse in the mouth. Tell me what else you'd like us to do together.''

Josie's stomach churned at the thought of being *that* honest. ''I...I don't think I can.''

''Why not?''

''It would be too...embarrassing.''

''That naughty, eh? Look, I doubt I can be shocked,

Josie. Not by anything sexual, anyway, except for
Clay's taking money for sex. That shocked me.''

"Maybe he only did it the once. Maybe he was
drunk. Kay said Cora was.''

"That's no excuse. I'm going to give him an earful
when I get home, I can tell you. But I'm not home
yet. I'm here with you and I want to know what's left
for me to do to you. I thought I covered most of the
Kama Sutra last night. So what other little fantasies
have been brewing inside that wildly wicked imagination of yours?''

Josie shrank from putting her personal fantasies into
words. But then she remembered that magazine.

"Wait here,'' she said, and jumped to her feet.

Callum waited and wondered exactly what Josie's
secret desires could possibly be? Clearly, they encom-
passed more than just straight sex. He hoped she didn't
want to be whipped. He wasn't into anything like that.
Callum *liked* women. He didn't want to humiliate or
hurt them. He didn't mind playing mild bondage
games. There was something very stimulating about
having a woman in a seemingly helpless state, especially when you knew that their seemingly being helpless turned them on to the ultimate degree.

Callum wasn't into being tied up himself, but he
could remember what it felt like to totally surrender
one's body to another person's will. He understood the
darkly delicious edge it brought to the experience. It
was just that he no longer enjoyed giving power over
his body, or his life, to another person, not even for a
little while. He liked to call the shots, sexually, and in
every other way.

"Here we are," Josie said as she hurried back into the room, ponytail swinging and silky robe clinging. She was holding what looked like one of those glossy women's magazines. Her big dark eyes were glittering and her nipples were like steel-tipped bullets.

"If you read the last three lists in this middle section," she said, handing the open magazine to him, "then you'll know the kind of thing I'd like to experience. Especially the last list. Not that I want to enact *every* one of the fantasies described. Some of them are pretty…um…daring."

Callum balanced the magazine on top of the things on the tray and quickly scanned the three lists. The first two were fairly standard sexual fare in his opinion. Josie had experienced pretty well everything in them with him last night, except for toe-sucking and a couple of the positions. The standing up one she'd only just missed out on. He'd definitely be doing that with her in the near future. Position five, however, was one even *he* hadn't tried. Mmmmm. Interesting. He'd put that in his memory bank and give it a go during the next nine nights.

Callum moved on to the third list which was the top ten favorite fantasies for women, number one being the most favorite in the survey. Each number had a headline against it which encapsulated the type of fantasy involved, followed by a few sample cases. Number one was SEX WITH A STRANGER.

Callum quickly realized that all of the fantasies listed weren't just about exotic sexual positions or kinky activities—though some had those as well—but sexual scenarios. They involved the brain as much as the body, each fantasy using different settings and various props to add an extra dimension to what was basically just straightforward sex between two trusting partners.

Well, perhaps not *quite* straightforward sex.

Callum was relieved, however, to see there wasn't any serious S & M involved, though yes, there was one bondage fantasy and another which involved spanking, something he'd never actually done to a woman. He wasn't sure how he'd react to doing that, even playfully. His body, however, seemed to like the idea, judging by the way it was responding to the thought of pulling Josie down across his lap right here and now, then pushing that scrap of blue satin up to expose her obviously bare butt.

In his mind's eye he could already feel her escalating tension as his palm came down hard onto her tautly held bottom. Her moans would be more pleasure than pain. Soon, she'd be begging him to stop, or to touch her there, between her legs, where she'd be soaking wet with desire and need.

"So what do you think?" she asked somewhat breathlessly from where she'd retreated again to the foot of the bed, looking faintly embarrassed yet obviously aroused. "You're not shocked, are you?"

Slowly, he shook his head, thinking it was just as well he had the tray across his lap. "Not at all."

A smile of relief filled her face. "Honestly?"

"Yes, honestly," he said while his eyes searched the list again. What fantasy included that spanking? Number three. Thankfully, he wouldn't have to wait too long for that one.

"You'd really like to try *all* of these fantasies, though, wouldn't you?" he suggested.

Her blush was so beautifully telling. "Well, I... I..."

"None of that prevaricating rubbish. You wouldn't have shown me this if it wasn't what you had in mind. We have nine more nights together before I have to catch my plane. There are ten fantasies, but if you recall, you've already done number one."

"I have?"

"Yep. Last night. SEX WITH A STRANGER. I was your stranger. That leaves nine fantasies and nine nights. One fantasy a night, working from two down to ten. Agreed?"

She looked poleaxed at first before licking her very sexy lips, then lifting her pointed little chin in a bold fashion. "Agreed."

Her agreeing sent a charge through him like a bolt of electricity. His flesh leapt some more, almost lifting the tray off his lap. He gripped the magazine more firmly and pushed down.

"Great. Now as much as I'd like to stay and rip that wrap right off you and ravish you silly, I'm going to get up and get dressed and go home. I have things to do there. I suggest you leave the hall stand up against the front door for now. You won't get a door man to come out on a Sunday. If you like, I'll arrange for it to be fixed on Monday while you're at work. You do have to go to work, don't you?"

"Unfortunately, I do," she said regretfully. "Kay needs my help all week to finish decorating the apartment for the auction next Saturday."

"That's fine. Give me the opportunity to rest up during the daytime. I have a feeling I might be needing it. I'll pick you up here at seven tonight. We're going out to dinner. Be ready."

"We're going *out?* But I thought...I mean..."

He smiled at her bewilderment.

"Fantasy number two is SEX IN A PUBLIC PLACE. That rather requires we go out somewhere, don't you think? Wear something accessible. No pants."

"No *pants?*"

"I meant no trousers, or jeans. But you're quite right. No panties is a very good idea as well. In fact, no underwear of any kind would be preferable. Wear a dress. Something soft and floaty."

Callum loved seeing the mixture of shock and excitement in her eyes. By the time seven o'clock came tonight, she'd be almost unbearably aroused.

And boy, she wouldn't be the only one!

13

"YOU'RE LATE," Deb reproached when Josie finally showed up at the harborside café where they'd agreed to meet for brunch that morning.

Josie dragged out a chair and sat down. "Only fifteen minutes." They were lucky she remembered to come at all. Ever since Callum left her shortly after ten-thirty, she'd been hard pressed to keep her mind on the present, and not on tonight.

Sex in a public place. What had she gotten herself into here?

"Well, come on, Josie," Lisa piped up impatiently. "We've been dying to know all about last night. You know, the reunion and everything."

"Yes, did you or did you not end up in bed with Angus?" Deb demanded to know.

"Huh?" Josie's thoughts were so full of Callum—and the night ahead—she'd forgotten momentarily that her roommates still believed she'd gone to the reunion with Angus.

"Yes, forget the reunion," Lisa agreed. "What we really want to know is all about the sex afterward."

The sex afterward. Oh dear, if only they knew...

But they weren't going to. Never in a million years. This was her private life, her private fling and yes, her private fantasies, about to come true. She wasn't going to spoil any of it by listening to Deb and Lisa's shock-horror reactions, followed by their do-you-really-think-you-should advice.

Josie was opening her mouth to launch into the story she'd already settled on—where Angus's departure from her life happened *after* he brought her home last night—when the sight of a smiling Brenda walking toward their table shocked her into further silence.

Panic was an understatement. Josie contemplated jumping up and dragging Brenda off to one side, but already it was too late.

"Fancy seeing you here this morning!" Brenda exclaimed as she stopped opposite Josie. "We haven't seen each other in five years and now it's been twice, in twenty-four hours. Look, I won't interrupt your lunch with your friends. I just wanted to say how lovely you looked last night and that I thought your Callum was everything you said he was."

Josie slid surreptitious eyes over at her roommates who'd picked up on the strange name and were exchanging frowns and faces. Deb mouthed *Callum* to Lisa and Lisa made a shrugging, eyebrow-raised gesture.

Fortunately, Brenda didn't draw breath long enough to let anyone get a word in.

"Could you pass a message on to Callum for me?" she rattled on. "Just say I'm going to take his advice and go blond. Amber thinks I'm crazy but I don't really care what she thinks. Frankly, I'm not going to see much of Amber anymore. She's not the person I thought she was. Do you know I found out she deliberately sent you an invitation without a note on it that you should bring it with you? I couldn't believe she'd stoop so low, just to embarrass you. Fancy being so petty and mean. Anyway, I just wanted you to know that I had nothing to do with it.''

"I'm glad," Josie said. "Thanks for telling me." She'd never really disliked Brenda. She'd just pitied her. Perhaps Callum had felt the same way. It had been sweet of him to encourage her to be her own person. And he was right. Brenda would look good as a blonde, and Josie told her so.

Brenda beamed. "I think so too. Like I said, I won't keep you," she added hurriedly when a waiter materialized by Josie's shoulder, wanting to take her drink order. "I'm meeting John at Doyle's at twelve-thirty for lunch so I'd better get a move on. You have a nice day now and give my love to Callum. Such a lovely man!" And she was gone.

Josie was grateful to be able to bury her head in the drinks menu. Much easier than having to face her two flabbergasted roommates.

But it was only a temporary reprieve, the waiter soon hurrying off to get her a glass of dry white wine.

"And who, pray tell, is Callum?" Deb asked in that frosty school-marm voice she sometimes used when she felt her friends had kept something from her.

No way was Josie going to tell them the truth, despite being found out to a degree. She'd just have to be more inventive.

"I didn't want to tell you girls the other night because I was still feeling so down about it, but Angus screwed up last Sunday night and I told him to go jump. I actually went to the reunion with this very nice fellow Kay knew and who kindly stepped in to pretend to be my boyfriend for the night. Luckily, I hadn't mentioned Angus's name when I said I was bringing my new boyfriend, so we got away with it. Everyone just assumed Callum was the boyfriend I'd boasted about.''

"Hey now, back up there a bit," Deb said, her expression still puzzled. "Just how *did* Angus screw up last Sunday night? If you tell me you *did* go to bed with him and he suffered from premature ejaculation or something like that, I won't believe you. Angus is sex on legs. And he knows it. No way would he be hopeless in bed like all your previous boyfriends.''

"Would you believe he was gay?''

"NO!" both girls chorused in forceful denial.

"Okay," Josie relented. "But he's bisexual. And that's just as much a non-starter in my book. We ran into an old lover of his.''

"Maybe he'd only been experimenting with guys," Lisa suggested generously. "Lots of men do that when they're young. He must go for girls more now, otherwise why ask you out in the first place?''

"He likes both," Josie said dryly. "At the same time, preferably. When he suggested a threesome with his previous male lover, I was out of there like a shot.''

"Golly, I don't blame you," Lisa said. "I mean… you'd have to be mad to go for that kind of scene these days.''

"Oh, I don't know," Deb said very ambivalently.

When Lisa and Josie both gave Deb a scandalized

look, she burst out laughing. "Only kidding. Josie did the right thing to ditch the bum. So tell us about this Callum guy. Is he single? Good-looking? What does he do? Did he like you? Has he asked you out again?"

"Whoa, Deb!" Lisa said, laughing now too. "Wait till the girl gets her drink or she'll run dry answering all those questions. But she's right, Josie, we both want to know absolutely everything about your date. This Callum sounds fab. Maybe your luck with men has finally turned."

Josie already knew that it had, to a degree, but not the way Lisa meant. Lisa was talking about meeting Mr. Right. Callum would never be that.

Josie contemplated lying and saying they hadn't liked each other that way and she was never going to see him again. But after running into Brenda out of the blue, she decided that was too risky a lie. What if she ran into Deb or Lisa when she was out with Callum? What could she possibly say to them?

No, she had to cover herself. So she opted for an edited version of the truth, telling them about Callum's age, career and single status, but emphasizing the fact that he was going back overseas soon and wasn't on the lookout for a girlfriend. He'd just been doing Kay a favor taking Josie to the reunion. Yes, he was good-looking, she admitted, and very nice. And yes, he had asked her out again. To dinner. Tonight.

"So soon?" Lisa said. "That sounds eager, Josie. I know you said he said he doesn't want a girlfriend and that he works overseas, but Sydney *is* his home. Australian guys always eventually come home to settle down, you know. Maybe he's lining you up as the girl he'll come home to.''

"That's pie-in-the-sky crap, Lisa," Deb said with her usual savage cynicism. "Some guys never settle down. They like playing the field too much. Josie's right. Callum McCloud is only good for a couple of dates and then he'll be off. Of course, if it was anyone other than Josie I'd say he'd be good for a few sex sessions as well. That's obviously why he's asking you out, Josie. I do hope you realize that there's no such thing as a free dinner date these days.''

"Yes, I do realize that, Deb," Josie said coolly, fed up with Deb thinking she was some kind of naive child in the dating game. "I'm a big girl now. I know what to expect. I can handle Callum." She certainly planned on handling him. A lot.

"Maybe, but you're not as tough as Lisa and me," Deb added. "You get hurt very easily."

"Do I look hurt about Angus?" Josie challenged.

"Well…no," Deb had to agree. "You look great. Actually, you look better than great. You're positively glowing. Why do you think she's glowing, Lisa?"

"Callum McCloud," Lisa replied smugly.

Josie laughed. "Truly, you two are the pits. And you're way off base. Trust me when I say there's no need to mollycoddle me with men anymore."

"Hmph!" Deb snorted. "You're still a babe in the woods where the opposite sex is concerned, so you be careful, girl."

"I'll be very careful," she promised. Which reminded her. Perhaps she should follow Deb's advice to the letter and get in a fresh supply of condoms. Deb always said you could never be too rich, too thin, or have too much protection.

Josie's glass of wine arrived and she was finally able to turn the conversation away from Callum and herself and onto what Lisa and Deb had been up to. But even as she pretended to listen to her friends' lively chatter, Josie's mind was focused on where it had been all day. Callum.

She started wondering where he was going to take her for dinner tonight and where he was going to have sex with her. She also wondered what he was doing right now, and if his head was as full of her, as her head was of him.

14

"You can't just fly off to L.A. like this," Callum roared at his brother. "It's crazy. You don't know what you're doing."

Clay slammed his suitcase shut and glared at his big brother. "I do know what I'm doing," he snapped. "I *am* going. And there's nothing you can do about it. The ticket is waiting for me at the airport, all paid for. A return ticket, might I add. So what's your beef? If things don't work out I can always come back."

Callum groaned and spun away, raking his hands through his hair as he tried to think of something to say to stop Clay from doing this. When he'd arrived home, Clay had been packing already. His announcement that the Hollywood executives had liked him a lot and wanted him to return to L.A. with them today for a screen test had totally distracted Callum from tackling Clay over the escort business. Saving his brother from making this new rash and rushed decision had become far more important.

"Look, are you going to drive me to the airport or not?" Clay asked. "If you won't, I can always get a taxi. But I need to know now. My flight leaves in just over two hours."

Callum whirled back to find Clay standing there

with his suitcase in hand and the most uncompromising steel in his long-lashed blue eyes.

"Well?" Clay prompted. "What's it to be?"

Callum expelled a ragged sigh. "I'll drive you," he said, sounding resigned but thinking to himself that this would give him some more time to talk Clay out of going.

Clay's smile stretched from ear to ear. "Thanks."

"When did you get yourself a passport?" was Callum's first question once they were under way. Clay had never been out of Australia before and would have had no need of one. Which was another reason Callum was worried. The boy had no experience of other countries and other cultures. L.A. could be a jungle, with lots of traps for an inexperienced pretty boy like Clay.

"I've had a passport since I was twenty-one," Clay confessed. "I wanted to be ready to go if and when opportunity knocked. And opportunity has knocked. In a *big* way. I still can't believe I'm going to Hollywood. It's a dream come true."

His dream and my nightmare, Callum thought, his mind full of all the potential disasters this trip could bring. Clay, not getting the part. His deciding to stay and audition further. His ending up doing escort work over there to make ends meet. Or worse. He'd already crossed the line at least once when it came to accepting money for sexual services. The second time would be much easier.

The right moment to approach Clay over what he'd done with that Cora woman had come. Fortunately, Callum was still in a position to preach, having used the robbery at Josie's home as an excuse to explain his not getting home till this morning. He'd told Clay he'd stayed the night at her place because the police had asked him to for safety and security reasons, which was technically true.

It had been slightly galling, however, that Clay had accepted this explanation without question. What kind of an undersexed wuss did Clay think he was? Fortuitous, though. Now he didn't have to give a do-as-I-say-not-as-I-do lecture.

"I need to talk to you about something," Callum said rather abruptly.

"Oh-oh. Here comes another lecture."

"Why do you say that?"

"You're using your big brother voice."

"Well, maybe it's called for. I'll have you know that I found out this morning you took money for sex from a recent client of yours, a woman named Cora. Is that right?"

Clay was completely shocked. "Geez, how did you find out about that?"

"So it's true!"

"Sort of," Clay muttered, his face mutinous.

"What do you mean sort of," Callum growled. "It either is or it isn't. You either did or you didn't."

"Okay, so I did."

"You had sex with her. *And* you demanded money for it the next morning?"

"Yes and no. I had sex with her all right. But I didn't demand money the next morning. I made some joke about the sex being an extra service which deserved a bonus, and the next thing I knew she was pressing some cash into my hands. I know I shouldn't have kept it but I had this huge cell phone bill and temptation got the better of me. That's the truth, Callum. Honest.''

"How many other clients have you had sex with?''

"None. I wouldn't have had sex with Cora except that I'd been pretending to be her boy-toy lover all night and it turned me on. On top of that she'd had a lot to drink. When I took her home she was all over me and before I knew it, we were doing it. I regretted it afterward but, geez, bro, haven't you ever done things you regretted?''

Callum didn't say a word.

"Probably not,'' Clay muttered under his breath. "Saint Callum. Never puts a foot wrong.''

Suddenly, Clay's head jerked round to stare at Callum. "Hey, wait a minute, how come you found out about all this? Who told you? Not that Josie girl. No way she knew about that. She wasn't the type to hire me in the first place. She was much too sweet.''

For a split second, Callum thought he was going to be hung by his own petard. But no, there *was* a way out.

"True, but she *was* the one who told me. It seems you were actually recommended to Josie by a close friend of hers called Kay, a cousin of Cora's to whom Cora had boasted of Beau Grainger's escorting and acting talents. Cora hadn't, however, said anything about the sex part, not till *after* she heard that Josie had hired you last night. When Josie called Kay this morning to tell her about the robbery, Kay blurted out the sordid details of your interlude with Cora. When

Josie confronted me with being some kind of gigolo over breakfast, I was forced to confess I wasn't Beau Grainger at all; that he was you and I was only standing in for you for the night.''

Clay crowed with laughter. ''I'll bet you had a heart attack there for a moment. The honorable Callum McCloud, being called a gigolo. That's just so funny!''

Funnier than he realized, Callum thought wryly. And almost true. Callum's mind catapulted back to how close he'd come to accepting Josie's check. Thank goodness he hadn't. Now he was really free to enjoy the sexual adventures he and Josie were about to embark upon together, without his conscience getting in the way.

He couldn't wait till tonight. His body stirred just thinking about it.

''At least now I know why you've been coming on hot and strong this morning,'' Clay said, breaking into Callum's rapidly heating train of thought. ''You're worried that I might sell myself over in L.A. if things don't work out as I hope. That's it, isn't it?''

''The thought had crossed my mind.''

''Look, Callum, I can tell you till I'm blue in the face that I won't do that, but I can't make you believe it. All I can say is that I'm not the backwater boy you think I am. Sydney is no longer a hick town, in case you haven't noticed. It's right up there with all the other major cities in the world. It has its good side and its bad side, its good guys and its bad guys. Trust me when I say I've already met plenty of the bad guys and I've survived. I'm not into drugs or gambling or orgies. And I'm not in the habit of selling myself. I told you. That was an accident and a mistake. So give me a break, will you, bro, and trust me for a change. I know that's hard for you to do. You've felt responsible for me since I was a baby and you just can't let go that feeling of responsibility. But it's time, Callum. Time to let go. I will survive. I can promise you that.''

Callum mulled over what Clay said for a while and was astounded to conclude that his kid brother was right. It *was* time to let go. Time for Clay to be thrown in the deep water to sink or swim. Callum couldn't be there, holding his head up all the time. No one had held *his* head up and yes, he had made mistakes and done things he'd regretted, but he'd learned from those mistakes and regrets. That was what growing up was all about. Clay deserved the opportunity to grow up by the same sensible if sometimes painful process.

"Just promise me one thing," Callum said. "If things don't work out with this part, then don't stay too long. Come back home."

"I can't promise that, Callum. Once over there, I'd have to stay a while and give Hollywood my best shot. Surely you can understand that. The return ticket is good for six months. I'll be using that six months to try to make my dream come true."

"Fair enough," Callum said through gritted teeth. "In that case, I'm going to put enough money into your bank account to cover your costs. A couple of thousand each month should do, but let me know if you need more."

Callum was staggered to see tears well up in his kid

brother's eyes. A lump formed in Callum's throat which threatened serious embarrassment.

"I can't tell you how much your doing that means to me, Callum," Clay said thickly.

"Then don't," came Callum's curt reply. Hell, they'd both be crying soon.

"You pretend to be tough, but you're a real softie underneath, aren't you?"

"Yeah, sure. That's me. A regular pushover. Just don't tell anyone."

"Who's there to tell?"

Callum thought of Josie and smiled. She wouldn't be interested in hearing he was a softie. She wanted him hard. Very hard.

Considering the way he twitched every time he even thought of her, Callum didn't think he'd have any trouble fulfilling that expectation, especially with what he had in mind for tonight.

Tonight...

She'd be shocked by what he was going to ask her to do. But he had no doubt that she'd do it. Josie was ripe and ready for sexual experimentation. She wanted to feel all there was to be felt. She wanted to wallow in her sexuality for a while, without the emotional constraints that a relationship sometimes put on the physical side of things. With him as her lover, she wouldn't have to worry about *his* pleasure at all. Her focus could be entirely on herself and her own satisfaction.

Josie claimed she'd never been satisfied the way Callum had satisfied her last night. Little did she know it but that was only the beginning. There was so much more for her to experience. Higher planes of arousal;

greater sexual awareness, especially of her own body; sharper levels of anticipation which naturally produced more intense orgasms.

She would be experiencing some delicious tension right now as time ticked slowly away toward their dinner date tonight. Anticipation always made time seem to go more slowly. Her awareness of her body would be heightened when she started to get ready; when she bathed in readiness for their night together; when she selected what dress to wear. But especially when she drew that dress over her beautiful, nude body which by then would be tingling and burning and aching for his touch.

But it would not be *his* touch which would first satisfy her by-then urgent needs.

Oh, no. Not his...

"I'll call when I get to L.A.," Clay said, breaking the silence in the car. "Put your mind at rest. But I won't be checking in every day or anything. Once a week will do."

"What? Oh yes. Once a week. Fine."

"Now for pity's sake stop worrying. I can hear the worry wheels going round and round in your head from here."

Callum laughed. What he was hearing wasn't worry but plotting and planning. It wasn't every day a guy had the opportunity to create nine fantastic sexual fantasies, then get to live them with the sexiest and most intriguing woman he'd ever met. Because let's face it, Callum, Josie was every *man's* fantasy come true.

No, perhaps not, he conceded. There were some men who liked the brainless blond bimbo type for a bed partner. Callum, however, liked his girlfriends to have brains. Because the brain was the most responsive erogenous zone. That was what made humans different from every other animal. Their brains. He aimed to turn Josie on and keep her turned on with her brain much more than her body.

"Okay," he told Clay. "I'll stop worrying."

"And for crying out loud have some *fun* for the rest of your break. Don't just go looking at boring old investment properties. Life's meant to be lived, bro. Get out and about for a change. Go to a singles bar. Pick up a girl. Get yourself laid."

"Okay."

Clay gaped over at him. "You mean that?"

"Sure. I'm no saint, Clay. Maybe it's time you realized that."

"Wow. This just gets better and better. I'm going to Hollywood. I have an allowance for six months. And my brother's going to get himself laid. Now don't forget to use protection, bro," he went on, amusing Callum with this sudden change of roles. Who was playing big brother now? "And don't listen to any girl who says she's on the pill. And keep your wits about you. There are some really good-looking girls who hang around the bars in Sydney who aren't girls, if you get my drift."

Callum laughed. "Don't worry, Clay. I'll keep my wits about me."

"Good. And don't go walking alone around the city after midnight. It's dangerous. You might get mugged. Take a taxi, even if it's only for a couple of blocks."

Callum threw his brother a disbelieving look, but at

least he had the comfort of knowing Clay wasn't the naive kid he'd been thinking he was. Both of them had misconceptions about each other. One day, Callum, decided, they were going to have a heart to heart and be honest with each other, the way he and Josie had been honest with each other this morning.

Aah…Josie…

Hard for his mind not to keep returning to her. God, but she was so beautiful, and so…sweet. Yes, Clay had been right about that. Josie *was* sweet, despite her being prepared to pay him for sex, and despite her wanting to experience all the sides of sex, including some of the kinkier ones. Callum had no doubt that once she'd experienced her ten fantasies for real, she wouldn't want to move on to wilder or kinkier scenarios. Basically, she just wanted her sexual curiosity—and her long-frustrated body—to be totally satisfied.

So tonight, after he showed her there was more to sex than just doing it, he was going to take her home to that lovely big empty house and make slow delicious love to her till dawn.

15

I CAN'T BELIEVE I'm doing this, Josie thought agitatedly as Callum led her through the restaurant in the wake of the very prim and proper maître d'.

Knowing that Callum knew she was naked under her dress was bad enough. The actual act of walking in her present highly aroused state was the real killer, her naked thighs brushing together, her bare buttocks being caressed by the silk lining of her dress.

Josie smothered the moan which threatened to escape. There wasn't a part of her body which didn't feel electrified. Blood was charging through her veins and her heart was going like an express train, running out of control with no brakes. She gritted her teeth in defiance of her dizzying excitement, but that only made the private parts of her body clench down hard as well.

Not a good idea if she was looking for control.

The tension gripping her insides became almost unbearable. She felt people looking at her, glancing up from their tables as she walked past. Could they guess she was totally nude under her dress, the dress she'd bought today especially for tonight because it was what Callum had commanded? A pale blue chiffon number with a scooped neckline and a flaring skirt which swished sexily around her legs. Did they know how wet she was between her legs, how desperate she was for a climax?

Her face flamed and her stomach curled over with shame. She couldn't do this. When her step faltered, Callum's hand gripped her elbow.

"Trust me," he whispered, then propelled her on.

Their table was in a private corner, a curved booth with black leather seats and a circular table with a single black candle in the centre of its elegant white linen tablecloth. The whole restaurant was decorated in black and white: white walls, black doors and trim, black and white tiled floor. In fact, that was what the restaurant was called. *Black and White.* The only relief from the stark décor was with the dim overhead lighting.

It was a fairly new place, tucked away in a back street of Neutral Bay. Josie had heard of it—it had received good reviews in the Sunday paper recently—but she'd never been here before.

The ladies' room, she noted, was just over to the right of them. Was that where Callum meant to take her to do it, she wondered? It had to be. There was nowhere else in here where they wouldn't be arrested. Or did he mean her to suffer through a meal then take her on somewhere else afterward? To a club, or a park, or who knew where. She shuddered at the thought of being pushed into some darkened doorway and ravished while people walked by. But she knew she wouldn't say no. *Couldn't* say no, she was so turned on.

Sliding into the booth and sitting down was another

torturous exercise, the seated position making her even more aware of her bare bottom, and where she feared the lining might now be sticking to her.

The maître d' was waffling on about the specials of the night but Josie couldn't concentrate on a word he was saying. She kept her eyes fixed on him, though. Much preferable to looking at Callum whom she suspected knew exactly how she was feeling.

He was a wicked devil, she decided. A *knowing* wicked devil. But oh so sexy. She'd thought he looked devastatingly attractive in his tux last night. But he looked better tonight, very rakishly handsome in black trousers and a cream silk shirt which was open at the neck and gave a glimpse of his beautifully hairy chest.

Josie had always thought she wouldn't like a man to have too much hair on his chest. She'd always recoiled before at the prospect of being smothered by a thick mat of wiry curls. But Callum's chest hair was quite soft and very sexy to touch. Just thinking about rubbing her rock-hard nipples through it made her press her thighs tightly together.

Oh, yes, she was very wet. Thank heavens her dress was lined or she'd have a damp patch when she stood up.

"What's wrong?" Callum asked softly when the maître d' finally departed with their orders.

His direct question forced her to look over at him.

"You know," she said stiffly, and he smiled.

"Don't you dare smile," she snapped, mortified. "This is just so embarrassing."

"But I'm only doing what you want, Josie," he said in an irritatingly cool voice. "Be honest. Ask yourself what you're *really* feeling. Are you cripplingly embarrassed or just unbearably excited? Genuinely afraid or exquisitely on the edge? If I said we'd get up and leave right now, would you go?''

''Yes,'' she hissed, and he laughed.

''Liar. You're sitting there, dying to know what I'm going to do to you. And where.''

He was right. She was. ''What…what *are* you going to do to me?'' she asked, her voice quivering along with her thighs.

CALLUM STARED deep into her large dilated eyes and felt his own control begin to slip. He hadn't been this excited in years. He'd been planning on waiting till she'd at least had a couple of glasses of wine before starting fantasy number two in earnest, but service in fancy restaurants like this was invariably slow and he simply couldn't wait to begin; to see how far he could push her; to see how much she would dare for him.

''Pull your dress up at the back,'' he said, sounding cool but feeling anything but.

''What?'' Her eyes blinked wide.

''Pull your skirt up at the back,'' he repeated quietly. ''Don't have anything between your bottom and the seat. Now don't panic,'' he hastened to add when it looked like she was going to do just that. ''We're in a very private dimly lit corner. The table is relatively high and the tablecloth reaches well down. No one can walk behind you and look down. No one will notice.'' A factor he'd taken into account when he booked this place and this table for tonight.

It had taken some research to find a restaurant which

had all the requirements he'd needed for this particular scenario but he'd managed it, courtesy of a restaurant site on the Internet which supplied virtual tours of the various venues. Callum had a feeling he'd be using the Internet a lot during the next nine nights, especially their online adult sites. There were lots of props he had to buy and little time to scour the city for them.

I CAN'T BELIEVE I'm doing this, Josie thought again as she did as Callum ordered. But ooh, the feel of the cool leather against her burning buttocks.

"Now pull your skirt up at the front to the top of your thighs. Then open your legs a fraction."

Josie's head began to swim. She did what he asked, her eyes glued to his like some lifeline.

"Wider, I think."

She moaned softly, but shifted her knees a few more inches apart.

"Now keep them like that," he commanded, and she sucked in sharply.

"But I can't, Callum," she protested shakily. "The waiter, he…he's coming with our wine. I can see him. He'll see me. He'll know."

"Cover your lap with your napkin. It's large enough."

She did, but her stomach churned and her heart raced the whole time the waiter stood by their table, opening the wine, pouring out the required taste for approval—over which Callum took his time—before carefully filling their glasses.

By the time he left them alone again, the whole surface of her skin was on fire.

"Pick up your wine," Callum said as he smoothly swept up his own glass. "No, with your left hand."

Startled, she did as he ordered. He clicked his glass against hers and once again, looked deep into her eyes, holding them with the power of his gaze. "Don't look away. Keep looking at me and keep sipping your wine."

She did, feeling both confused and mesmerized.

"Now remove the napkin and start touching yourself. And don't go telling me you've never done that before. A girl as highly sexed as yourself must have done it for herself before tonight."

He was right. She had. But not often and only in the total privacy of her bedroom or bathroom. To do it here, in front of him, and in front of all these other people…

Was it thrills or chills which rippled down her spine?

"I…I can't," she choked out.

His eyes stayed steady. "You can and you will."

Could she? Would she?

Apparently so.

She was so wet it was unbelievable. But once she started she couldn't stop. Her lips gasped apart. She tried hiding her gaping mouth with the wineglass, but it was useless. Her teeth clinked against the rim and she almost spilled her wine.

The only decorum she achieved was silence, but it was such a struggle to stifle her moans and keep her breathing from deteriorating into ragged panting. Nothing, however, could stop the wave of heat from washing over her skin, or the goose bumps which sprang up on her arms. She was afraid that people were staring at her but she dared not check. It took all of her willpower to try to look normal, even as she was bringing herself closer and closer to an orgasm which threatened to blow her mind. Oh yes, she knew what that meant now. This climax had been building all day. It was going to be fierce, and she was going to have it here, in a restaurant, in front of all these people, in front of Callum who was sitting there sipping his wine and looking oh so cool.

When her face twisted into a pre-orgasmic grimace, she moaned his name and threw him a pleading glance.

In the time it took to blink an eye, he'd put down his wine and slid along the seat to be right beside her. Whipping her glass away, he captured the nape of her neck with one hand while his other dived down between her legs, covering hers and pressing her hand hard against her burning clitoris. It was enough to tip her over the edge.

CALLUM'S MOUTH CRASHED down on hers just in time. But he could feel her spasms all through him and he almost came himself. Fortunately, he didn't and he kept kissing her till she stopped shaking. But it was the most difficult thing he'd ever done.

Still, it was worth it to see the look in her eyes when his head finally lifted. Not just physical satisfaction— though he suspected that had been considerable—but intellectual satisfaction as well. Now she knew that the joys of sex had many and varied faces. Now she wouldn't fight his wishes during the next eight days.

She'd be eager to experience whatever other previously unknown pleasures were in store for her. She'd be his to command.

His.

He liked that thought.

When Callum lifted both their hands away from her temporarily sated flesh, she sank against him in the sweetest of surrenders. Gently, he pushed her legs back together and smoothed her skirt down over her knees. Kissing her lightly on the forehead, he slid back to his spot, and his glass of wine, and his own personal agony of waiting till later.

But oh, that later was going to be something. She didn't know it yet but the orgasm she'd just experienced was just a taster, an appetizer so to speak for the main course. And dessert. The night was still very young.

"That was...incredible," she told him later over their dinner, her face still slightly flushed. "Did you like it too?" she asked. "Watching me, I mean."

Callum was momentarily taken aback. He was the one supposed to be asking the questions, not her. Still, he supposed it was only natural for an intelligent girl like Josie to want to know what her partner felt as well.

"It was...stimulating," he admitted dryly.

"But not satisfying, like it was for me."

"If you're asking if I came, then no, of course not."

"Why of course not? I couldn't have stopped myself coming if I tried. What would happen if I asked you to touch yourself like that here? Or what if I slid over and touched you myself under *your* napkin. Would you come?''

Like a shot, came the appalling thought.

''Would you be prepared to do that?'' he asked, deflecting her question with his, and thinking smugly that she wouldn't.

Her head tipped to one side and a swathe of glossy black hair fell forward over her shoulder. It was mostly down tonight, only the sides brushed back from her face and anchored with very feminine silver clips. Her whole attire was very feminine, and didn't betray her nakedness underneath.

''Yes, I would,'' she confessed, ''if *you* wanted me to.''

Callum gulped. She was tempting him all right. But getting his rocks off under this table was not what he wanted.

''I'm saving it up,'' he murmured. ''For later.''

''Oh. I…I thought that was it. Fantasy number two all complete.''

''Don't you want there to be a later?''

''Silly question,'' she said, and smiled a smile that sent his already straining erection into serious overload. ''I only have your services for nine more nights. I'm certainly not going to settle for one miserable little orgasm. I know you're good for a whole lot more than that.''

Callum laughed. ''You're turning into a very naughty girl, do you know that?''

''If I am, then you have only yourself to blame. You're corrupting me.''

Callum laughed again. ''*Me*, corrupting *you? You're*

the one who shoved that magazine article in my face. *You're* the one who wants a walk on the wild side."

"And you don't?" she challenged.

"Honey, in the state I'm in at the moment, I'd be lucky to walk anywhere."

"Oh," she said, the color zooming back in her face. But her eyes were glittering and her lips stayed provocatively apart. "Couldn't I feel it a little bit?"

"You can feel it all you like for as long as you like...*later.*"

"Spoilsport."

Now her lips were pouting sulkily. God, but she had the sexiest mouth. Full and lush. Glossed a bright pink as her lips were tonight, they would look incredible wrapped around his penis.

He would have her that way first. She wouldn't say no. He could hardly wait.

Already Callum suspected nine nights might not be enough. He'd be strongly tempted to look her up again the next time he was in Sydney.

Of course, by then it was possible Josie wouldn't want to see *him* again. She might have found herself a new boyfriend, one who fully concurred with what she wanted out of life this time.

Callum frowned over the image of Josie with some other man. He didn't like it much. Actually, he didn't like it at all!

But that was typical of any male animal, he accepted. They were by nature possessive creatures, especially sexually. They were programmed that way for the survival of the species. Programmed to protect, too.

It worried Callum that some unscrupulous man might come into Josie's life after he'd left and exploit her newfound sexuality. As much as *he* rejoiced in her blossoming sensuality, a lot of men might take ruthless advantage of it.

He vowed to subtly warn her of such men during the coming nights; to make her aware of never letting herself be open to abuse. Erotic games could be fabulous fun, but they could also be dangerous in the wrong hands. There had to be a lot of trust between the couple involved. And a lot of genuine affection, especially on the man's part.

Callum liked Josie a lot. She was a darling. But she was also a little bit naive. She shouldn't really be trusting him so much and so quickly. What did she know of him, really?

Not much.

At the same time, he didn't want to spoil her pleasure in their fling. Obviously, she needed to do this; needed to explore her sexuality and put aside all her past uptight experiences in favor of some newer and less inhibited ones. She needed to feel confidence and pleasure in her body, not worry and insecurity. She needed satisfaction, not frustration. She needed…him.

Callum smiled to himself. It was a tough job but someone had to do it.

16

"JOSIE, WHAT ON EARTH is wrong with you today?" Kay grumbled. "I leave you to do the simplest tile painting job and I come back half an hour later to find you standing here in this kitchen, daydreaming, with the paintbrush as stiff as a patio broom? This is not the way to get this apartment finished for the auction this Saturday. We have the bathroom tiles to do yet, not to mention countless other time-consuming little jobs!"

"Sorry. Didn't get much sleep last night."

"Here, Give me that paintbrush." Kay dumped it into the tin of turpentine then peered into her boss's eyes. "You don't look tired."

When Kay had first seen Josie this morning, dressed in tight blue hipster jeans and a bright pink stretchy top which showed off her great figure, she'd thought wow!

Even with a closer inspection, Kay could find nothing to criticize. Her eyes were clear and bright, though somewhat distracted in expression.

"Is there something wrong, Josie? You know you can tell me anything."

Josie looked at Kay and thought, yes, she simply

had to tell *someone,* and who better than Kay who was wise and sensible and sympathetic?

So she told her. Everything. Well...*almost* everything, from the moment Callum had picked her up on Saturday night till she'd left him behind at her parents' house this morning to organize the new door. The bit she left out was their decision to play out the remainder of the ten fantasies together, saying instead that Callum had offered her a strictly sexual fling till he went back overseas. Nights of undiluted sex, the kind Josie had always dreamed of sharing with a lover but which she'd never experienced before.

Since she wanted Kay's honest advice, it seemed important not to water down her own behavior too much, so Josie admitted going without her underwear during her dinner date last night, but left out what she'd done there in that restaurant. That was much too private—and much too embarrassing—to confess to.

Even so, Kay had looked quite shocked to begin with. Then very thoughtful. And irritatingly silent.

"*Say* something," Josie insisted.

"Mmmm," she said, which wasn't much help.

Kay looked at Josie and simply didn't know where to start. She couldn't have been more surprised—all this, from a girl whom she'd thought was uptight about sex!

"You're not disgusted with me, are you?" Josie asked, her lovely eyes anxious.

"Disgusted? Why would I be disgusted?"

"Peter called me a pervert for years. Said a nice girl shouldn't want to do what I wanted to do with him."

Now Kay was appalled. What kind of weirdo had

that husband of hers been to take that attitude? But at least she now understood Josie's seemingly prim and proper attitude to sex. She'd been programmed that way.

"Don't be ridiculous, Josie. You're a perfectly normal female with perfectly normal desires. That ex of yours was the pervert, in my opinion. He should have been thanking his lucky stars to have a wife like you who likes and wants sex. Just as well you divorced him. But back to the problem at hand, which I presume is Callum McCloud."

Kay watched Josie blush. The girl had it bad this time, she realized. Much worse than when she'd been seeing Angus. If she wasn't careful she was going to get really hurt. But how could Kay tell her not to see this Callum again? He was clearly delivering what she'd never had before. And delivering it big time!

No, Kay decided, there was no point in telling Josie to stop this affair right now. She'd just see him anyway and not tell Kay. Girls in serious lust—which Josie obviously was—didn't take such advice. All Kay could do was to make sure Josie would be careful and not take any risks regarding pregnancy or her health. Because Josie was going to fall in love with the dashing Mr. McCloud. That was a foregone conclusion under these circumstances. Of course, Mr. McCloud would not suffer a similar fate in return. He'd already stated his case, with blunt but creditable honesty. Kay had to give him that. He wasn't giving Josie the runaround. He was, however, a committed bachelor with no intentions of settling down. Not the sort of man for Josie. Kay had to make sure her friend continued to see the guy in that way and not go putting on any rose-tinted spectacles.

Now where to start? Somewhere not too confrontational…

"So Deb and Lisa think *I* organized this Callum to take you to the reunion and that now you're dating him till he goes back overseas next week."

Josie gnawed away at her bottom lip. "I…er… didn't tell them I was dating him, exactly. I admitted to one dinner date last night because after running into Brenda like that yesterday, I didn't want to get caught out again. I had no idea at that time where Callum was taking me for dinner, and if Deb and Lisa had seen me out with some strange guy without telling them, there'd have been hell to pay."

"This probably is off the point, but why haven't you told them the truth, like you just told me? I mean…you are best friends, aren't you?"

"Yes. And I love them dearly. But they are both a little silly when it comes to men. They complain ad infinitum about the opposite sex while they're boy-friendless, but a good-looking guy has only to give either of them the eye and they're in bed with them before you can say boo. I know exactly what they'd say if I told them the truth about Callum and me. They'd say go for it, girl, without thinking of the risks, or the regrets afterward."

"I see," Kay asked, pleased to hear that Josie still had her wits about her. Clearly, she wasn't madly in love with the man as yet. "And *are* you regretting what you've done with Callum?"

"No," Josie said pensively. "No, I'm not. And I think *that's* the problem. Shouldn't I be?"

"Why? From the sounds of things he's just what the doctor ordered. An experienced stud who knows women and what turns them on. I presume he was the one who suggested the no knickers business? No, don't bother to deny it, I can see by your face that he did. And no, I'm not shocked, or disgusted. I've been there, done that myself."

"Really?" The relief on Josie's face was evident.

Kay decided what Josie needed from her more than anything was not to be shocked by what she said, or did. Clearly, the girl needed this fling. She'd been repressing her sexuality for far too long.

"The first time Colin suggested I go without my underwear in public," Kay said blithely as she turned her attention to cleaning the paintbrush, "I almost went crazy, especially when he made me walk around town with him that way. It was a windy night and my skirt kept blowing up. I felt so wicked, yet sooo sexy. He went crazy in the end too," she continued with a remembered laugh. "All of a sudden he pulled me into a movie theatre and really went to town with me. Thank goodness the movie was one of those noisy action flicks because we weren't very quiet."

Josie was both taken aback and relieved by Kay's confession. She laughed, but then frowned, worry regathering. "Yes, but you and Colin were probably engaged at the time. It occurred to me this morning that I don't really know Callum all that well."

"Yes, you do," Kay said, a cheeky sparkle in her

eyes. "You know him *very* well, from what I've just heard."

"That's not what I mean and you know it."

"True. Look, if you insist on seeing this situation on the very serious and extra sensible side, I still say you know him *quite* well already. A man is known by his actions, Josie. This Callum might be a confessed Casanova, but at heart, he's also a decent man. You think about it. A bad guy wouldn't have been so darned nice to you at your reunion. And a bad guy would have taken your money when you offered it the next morning, then taken you for a total ride instead of being brutally honest. No, I don't think you have to worry about Callum's basic character. He won't deliberately hurt you. The danger in this affair, if there is one, is your falling in love with him. So tell me…is that what's really worrying you this morning, Josie? That you might be falling for him already?"

Josie could not have been more stunned. "Falling for a man who's already told me he'll never settle down and marry or have children? Oh, no! No, I won't be doing that. I'm not that stupid. I guess I was just worried that I was taking risks in being so intimate and trusting with some stranger. But I see now that he's not a stranger at all. You are so right, Kay. I know more about him already than I ever knew about Angus. As much as I made it sound like Callum and I spent all last night doing it, we actually did quite a bit of talking as well."

"Mmmm." Kay gave her a very dry glance. "That's your story and you're obviously going to stick with it."

"It's true!"

"So what did you talk about?" Kay went back to cleaning the poor pathetic paintbrush which was on the verge of dying and going to paintbrush heaven.

"Oh, lots of things. Books. Movies. His job. My job. His family. My family. Did you know his brother flew to Los Angeles yesterday to have a screen test for some hot-shot Hollywood director? I hope he makes it. Callum hopes so too. He's tired of being his brother's keeper. His father walked out on them when Callum was six and Clay was just a baby, so he's been responsible for Clay ever since. More so after his poor mother ended up dying from a brain tumor."

"Heavens, but that's terrible!" Kay shook her head. Some people had such tragic lives. Still, perhaps Callum's burdensome background explained why he didn't want to take on the responsibility of a wife and family. "When did that happen?"

"I'm not sure when. A few years back, I think. That's one subject Callum won't talk about. His mother. He only mentioned her death in passing when I asked him about his parents."

"For a couple who are having a strictly sexual liaison," Kay said quietly, "you sure are exchanging a lot of personal information." Could she be wrong about this pair having some chance together? Stranger things had happened....

"What? Oh, no, it's nothing like that. But you have to talk about something when you're...er...um..."

"Lying there, waiting for his joy stick to recover?"

"Kay! Don't be so crude!" Josie exclaimed, but her eyes were laughing. "Besides, it's me mostly who has to recover. Callum's…er…joy stick seems to operate on auto pilot. It does come down to land occasionally, but before you know it, it's up, up and away again.''

''Lucky you. Okay, so what's Callum got lined up for you both tonight?''

Josie couldn't help coloring guiltily, but fortunately Kay had returned to cleaning the paintbrush and wasn't looking at her. ''He's coming over to my place, if that's what you mean. I've offered to cook him dinner.''

''In the nude?'' Kay said casually, then glanced up with a devilish smile on her impish face.

Josie was speechless. How had she guessed? Fantasy number three was the master and servant girl scenario, with Callum suggesting exactly what Kay had guessed, despite it not being one of the examples in the magazine. Callum had said he wasn't going to follow any of those exactly. He was going to fashion their fantasies especially for them.

''Don't forget to wear an apron,'' Kay said with experience in her voice. ''Cooking in the nude has a lot of hazards. Oh, and if you decide to use oil during sex at any time, then for pity's sake put something on the bed which you can throw away afterward. You just can't get that darned stuff out of the sheets.''

''I hadn't thought about oil yet,'' Josie murmured. But she started thinking about it straightaway. Tomorrow night was the woman on top fantasy, which meant a woman-in-charge scenario, not just a sexual position. That was the only fantasy where she had total control, and despite it not being her favorite fantasy— she much preferred the man to be dominant—the idea of Callum lying back while she gave him an all-over massage was very appealing. Just the thought gave her goose bumps.

"You will," Kay said confidently. "Colin and I were constantly experimenting with sex when we first met. You know, different positions and things. We worked our way through every position known to mankind and tried all the usual sex toys and lots of other lovely kinky stuff. Crotchless panties, leather corsets, mirrors, handcuffs."

"Handcuffs!" Josie exclaimed, her mind propelling her straight to the bondage fantasy. Which number had that been? Number seven, she thought. That wouldn't be for a while yet. As much as her excitement level zoomed at the idea of being handcuffed to a bed, that kind of scenario required enormous trust.

"You don't fancy being handcuffed?" Kay asked. "It's incredibly sexy."

"I...I think it's too risky."

"Yes, you could be right. Colin and I didn't try that till after we were engaged. No, don't agree to being handcuffed, or tied up, or anything like that just yet."

"I won't." But even as she said that she wouldn't, Josie suspected she just might, after she knew Callum a little longer, and that decision was a few days off yet.

Josie scooped in a deep breath then let it out slowly.

Talking to Kay had been good for her peace of mind, but talking about Callum and sex was not good for the peace of her body. Only three days she'd known him and already she was addicted to the pleasure he could give her. She lived for the moments when they were together. Nothing else seemed important. Not her work, or her company, or even her friends. When Deb and Lisa called her last night just as she and Callum walked in the door after dinner, she'd swiftly used an excuse to get them off the phone so she could return to her fantasy world. And Callum.

But before she'd hung up on her friends she'd agreed to meet them as usual at their favorite bar this Wednesday night after work. Josie's permanently turned-on body now fiercely regretted that promise, but her more sensible brain knew that by Wednesday, it would be a wise thing to have a break from Callum, to take a breather from what they'd been doing. Wednesday night's fantasy was the sex-with-a-man-in-uniform fantasy which didn't really do all that much for her anyway, despite her having adored Richard Gere in *An Officer and A Gentleman*. If she had to give up one of the fantasies, then that would be her choice. Telling Callum tonight that she couldn't see him on Wednesday night would be difficult, but it had to be done.

Kay's warning about not falling in love had really struck a chord with her. It would be so easy to surrender herself, body *and* soul, to that man. He was everything she'd ever dreamt about. And more.

But falling for Callum was a sheer waste of her time, and would only lead to emotional pain. And she'd had enough emotional pain in her life so far. So she aimed to keep her head. And if that meant exercising a bit of self-control and not indulging herself in every single one of those fantasies, then so be it!

Kay's voice broke into her thoughts. ''You know,

Colin and I have got into a bit of a rut lately with our sex life,'' she said as she finally finished cleaning Josie's paintbrush. "Talking to you today has given me an idea. The poor love's been shockingly stressed out at work lately. Gets home positively exhausted each evening. Obviously, what he needs is a nice long relaxing bath followed by an all-over massage, followed by…''

"I think we should get on with this painting, don't you?'' Josie said, knowing that if she didn't bring a stop to all this sex talk she'd be back to being hopeless for the rest of the day. "Like you said, Kay. There a hell of a lot to do here yet. Though what you've done already has made a world of difference. You are a genius, no doubt about that.''

Kay preened as she glanced around the bright white kitchen which was as different from the old kitchen as day was to night. "I am, aren't I?''

"You seem to know exactly what colors to paint a room,'' she said glancing over at the cool green on the living room walls.

"It's only common sense really, and a touch of Feng Shui. I choose colors that blend and don't offend. White is always safe for kitchens and bathrooms, but I always use the paler shades of blue or green for the rest of the rooms. I never use hot or bright colors on walls. No red, orange, pink, purple or yellow. And no black. Ever. I hate black in a house. But of course, it's the placement of the furniture and accessories which is the most important factor. And keeping things uncluttered and simple.''

"Whatever, it works, Kay. When the people walk

through here on inspection day, they're going to fall in love with this place.''

"Enough to part with half a million dollars?''

Josie refused to be daunted by that reserve price. She wasn't flattering Kay. The unit was already looking fantastic. And it didn't even have any furniture in it yet.

"More,'' she said confidently. "Much more.''

"Much more?'' Kay laughed. "I said I was a genius, not a miracle worker. But I sure hope you're right. Come on, then, let's get on with it.''

17

CALLUM HAD BEEN QUITE SURE, when he'd first looked at that list of fantasies, that tonight's fantasy, the woman-on-top scenario, was not going to be *his* personal favorite. But given it was only one out of a number of other very exciting scenarios, then he'd been prepared to endure it for Josie's sake.

He'd also agreed to do whatever she asked. Which was fair enough, given she'd done everything he'd asked the night before. But when he'd made that faithful promise Callum had pictured her wanting him to do things like suck her toes, give oral sex for ages or lie back passively...

Well...he was finally lying back passively on the bed which was covered by some funny old dust-sheet for some reason, but so far the evening had not progressed as he'd imagined. Hell, not even close!

First, she'd ordered him to strip totally as soon as he arrived at her front door around seven, a request that he'd found oddly embarrassing. Odd because it had never bothered him being naked in front of Josie before.

Perhaps his discomfort originated in her remaining fully dressed, and looking exquisitely sexy in skin-tight white jeans and a lacy black shirt with no bra on underneath. Seeing her pretty pink nipples peeking out at him through the semi-sheer top had been enough to give his already aroused flesh an added boost, something which was painfully obvious without any clothes on.

Yet despite the degree of mortification which accompanied his then being directed to follow her down the steps into the living room like some sex slave, an undeniable excitement had gathered in the pit of his stomach as well. Even more so when she commanded him to stand in the middle of the room and stroke himself while she settled back on a couch opposite with a glass of chilled white wine to sip and watch.

Callum, whose male pride demanded he not show the slightest hesitation or inhibition, had complied with her wishes, despite suspecting he would soon be on the edge of total embarrassment.

Which had been the case.

Josie's giggling saved him. It was very hard to come while the woman watching you was so patently amused. She'd giggled the night before too when he'd pulled her down across his lap to pretend-punish her for spilling a single drop of his wine.

Her laughing at his spanking her was not exactly the erotically charged scenario Callum had had in mind at the time. When he'd landed a seriously smarting slap across her deliciously bare buttocks, she'd stopped laughing, turning her head to throw the most smoldering look up over her shoulder at him.

"That really hurt," she'd said, her voice low and sexy. "I think you should kiss it better, don't you?"

From that moment, things had gone more or less according to his plan.

Tonight, however, had not gone to plan at all. Because of course it wasn't his plan. It was hers, damn it all. If he'd been the one in charge, he wouldn't have stood there, obediently touching himself. He'd have had her on her knees before him. Or on her hands and knees. And *she'd* have been the one naked, not him.

The ringing of the doorbell right in the middle of this fiasco had provided Josie with even more amusement. She'd made him answer the door with nothing but a tea-towel tied around his hips, while she'd killed herself laughing behind the door. Goodness knew what the poor pizza delivery guy thought.

But that wasn't the worst of it. She'd then poured herself a bubble bath and made him kneel beside the tub and wash her very slowly all over.

During this mind-altering activity, she'd fed him only the tiniest bites of the pizza while she'd devoured the rest.

"Male sex slaves," she'd told him cheekily when he dared to complain, "have to be kept hungry to perform well."

He'd been hungry all right. By the time she told him to stop washing her, he'd been ravenous. For *her*.

At last, he'd thought, when she climbed out of the bed, her beautiful body all rosy and soft from the water, pebbly nipples poking through the soap bubbles.

But no, his torture had hardly begun. He'd been commanded to dry her all over, slowly, dabbing at her inch by inch with a towel, forbidden to touch her flesh directly with his hands. It had been the same when she'd been in the tub. He'd had to keep the sponge between his hand and her skin at all times. She'd shuddered convulsively when he'd dried her between the legs but it hadn't been a full-blown orgasm. Just one of those tiny little climaxes which primed a woman rather than satisfied her.

Once dried to her satisfaction, she'd sat down at the dressing-table back in the bedroom—in the nude—and he'd had to brush her hair. For simply ages!

And all the while she'd chattered away to him like he was some hairdresser, telling him about the day she'd spent painting the bathroom tiles white in that apartment she and Kay were fixing up. She'd also mentioned how she'd dropped in the list of stolen items to the police station on the way home and how she'd received the insurance claim form in the mail, along with a postcard from her parents. They were in Paris.

As if he cared!

At that point, she'd asked him if he'd heard from Clay and he'd informed her through clenched teeth that his brother had sent an e-mail when he arrived in L.A. and would be calling him this weekend. Though probably not. Clay was not renowned for keeping in touch.

The *coup de grâce* of this largely one-sided conversation, however, had been her coolly informing him that she was foregoing the next fantasy tomorrow night because she had a standing date to meet Deb and Lisa every Wednesday night and she didn't want to let her friends down.

Josie's adding that she'd never fantasized over having sex with a guy in uniform anyway did not lessen the impact this news had had on Callum. He'd been thinking about the nights to come nonstop. Every second of every day was consumed by planning them. And now she wanted to skip one. He'd even picked up the uniform from a costume rental shop!

But she'd been adamant about her decision and there was nothing he could do about it.

By the time she'd told him to stop brushing her hair and lie down on the bed, Callum had been totally frustrated, both physically and emotionally. How he'd stopped himself from simply throwing *her* on the bed then himself on top of her, he had no idea. His control amazed him sometimes.

Her control was amazing him too. Not to mention her sexual deviousness. The girl was the devil incarnate tonight. Yet she could be an angel too. He wasn't surprised that she was a Gemini. She definitely had two sides. The trouble was he liked both personalities. The softly sweet Josie who melted under his kisses and let him do whatever he pleased, and the teasing, tormenting creature he'd met tonight.

Callum knew which woman he preferred.

Thinking such thoughts calmed him somewhat. Which was good, since tonight Josie hadn't joined him on the bed but disappeared back into the bathroom with an airy "I won't be a moment."

Ten minutes later, she still hadn't made a reappearance. She was playing the dominatrix with amazing skill, and to amazing effect.

The sound of the bathroom door finally being opened sent an erotically charged shudder all through his body. Talk about torture and pleasure combined! There was nothing more exciting, he realized, than the bittersweet excitement of being made to wait for one's satisfaction. Callum had long known how to use anticipation to good effect on a woman. But no woman had ever exercised the same technique so successfully on him, till Josie.

"Sorry to be so long," she said as she swept back into the room. Her skin was shiny and slippery-looking, like she'd rubbed some kind of oil all over it. Whatever it was, it smelled exotic. Her hair was up out of the way in a twist and her mouth had been glossed a bold red.

"I see you've been a good boy while I've been gone," she remarked, feasting sparkling eyes on his outstretched body, especially that part of him which would not lie down.

His mouth dried as he stared at the small green glass bottle she had in her hands.

"What's that?" he asked out when she placed it on the nearest bedside table.

"Just some lotion I bought today from one of those shops which specializes in aromatherapy oils. All made from natural products and good for you," she added as she coolly climbed up onto the bed and straddled him around his thighs, giving him a view which reversed his earlier calm, and made him shudder again, all over.

Her action in then leaning right up over his body to pick the bottle up again was clearly designed to torment him further, her oiled breasts brushing against the tip of his erection as she did so.

A sound was torn from Callum's throat, which brought her eyes snapping to his.

Shining eyes. Excited eyes.

"This particular body rub is reputed to act as an aphrodisiac," she murmured. "It's also edible. I thought that was important, considering where it's going to end up."

He moaned.

"Poor baby," she crooned and poured a large pool of the lotion into his navel. "Don't worry. I'll put you out of your misery soon. Just be patient a little longer...."

He moaned again when she dripped some more lotion onto each nipple, then onto his scrotum, but not where he most desperately wanted it.

"I can't take much more of this, Josie. I'm only a mortal man."

"But such a beautiful mortal man," she purred, her hands sliding all over him, spreading the oily lotion far and wide. "There are times when I just want to grab you and hold you tight and eat you all up."

Callum knew what she meant. He felt the same way about her. The difference between them at this precise moment was that she was doing it.

He watched, his gut twisting as she took hold of his by now glistening penis and eased it in between her ruby-red lips, sucking him down deep, then deeper, then deeper still. His head spun and the blood roared through his body. He couldn't think anymore. He didn't want to think. He just wanted to let go, to surrender to the wet heat of her mouth and the ecstasy promised within.

Yet he feared such a surrender and tried to resist, tried to hang on. "Josie," he cried out when his climax became imminent. "No, stop. I..."

But it was too late for such feeble protests, too late to stop his body from giving in to its primal urgings.

"Aaaaah," he cried out as all resistance ceased, and his body and soul entered the mindless rapture of total surrender. He was hers, to do with as she willed.

And he no longer cared.

18

THE BAR WHERE the girls met every Wednesday night at seven was only a short walk from the old house they shared at Milsons Point. It was small and dark, yet had a warm and intimate atmosphere.

The girls had a favorite table which the barman was good enough to keep reserved for them. And why not? They were regulars and no trouble at all. Josie was a little late, *again,* but Deb and Lisa forgave her because they knew she'd had to drive from Manly and that light drizzle that day had made the traffic a nightmare. Not that it wasn't always a nightmare anywhere near the bridge around that time.

By eight, they'd devoured their hamburgers and chips, along with a couple of light beers, and had got down to some serious gossiping about men and sex. At least, Deb and Lisa had. Josie had more reasons than usual to tread lightly on the subject for fear of tripping up and somehow revealing that her fantasy world was now very much her real world. Her *only* world at the moment. She couldn't seem to think about anything else but Callum, and the fantastic sex they'd been sharing. Kay had been complaining during the day about how distracted she'd been.

"Hey! Hey you!" Deb said, snapping her fingers right in front of Josie's face.

Josie blinked. "What?"

"Lisa asked if Callum had called you since she last talked to you on the phone. When was that, Lisa? Sunday?"

"Yep."

"Well? Has he?"

"Has he called?" Josie repeated, frowning.

Deb rolled her eyes. "It isn't a trick question, Josie. Has…he…called?" she repeated slowly as one would to an idiot. "On…the…telephone."

"No, not yet," she said, and it wasn't a lie. She'd asked him not to phone her, part of her desperate effort to keep some control over this situation. Though he'd told her before leaving her last night that he *would* be calling her some time tomorrow, since the fantasy on the list was the call girl scenario.

"Bummer," Lisa said. "I was hoping he would."

"Nah, I knew he wouldn't," Deb said. "Josie doesn't put out. If a girl doesn't put out by the second date these days, guys like Callum never call back."

"What do you mean by guys like Callum?" Josie said far too defensively. "He's a really nice guy."

"Just listen to her, getting all sweet about some man she's only seen twice and will never see again. Girl, get a grip! Swinging singles like your Callum have only one interest in a female and it has nothing to do with their brains. If they don't get a poke, or at least a blow job after paying for a fancy dinner, they don't call back. End of story."

"I don't believe that," Josie said crossly, though

who knew why she felt so angry? Deb was probably right, even about Callum, because Josie had well and truly put out this time. *And* given him the best blow job in the entire world last night.

Callum wasn't spending each night with her for her brains. Or her scintillating conversation. Or because he'd fallen madly in love with her. It was for the sex. She'd known that from the start. So why start hoping for a change in his motives at this stage?

Perhaps because she was beginning to worry that her own motives—and feelings—were changing. She'd told Kay earlier this week that she wouldn't be stupid enough to fall in love with the man, and she sure hoped she wasn't. But, oooh, she was missing him tonight. Terribly.

She hadn't felt this edgy, or this uptight, since she'd given up smoking a few years back.

"Yes. That's it!" she suddenly exclaimed, and sat up straight in her chair. What she was suffering from wasn't love, Josie realized, but something similar to withdrawal from an addiction. Callum was making her addicted to sex every night. Not just ordinary sex, either. Blindingly brilliant multi-orgasmic sex. Her body was being programmed to crave half a dozen climaxes, every twenty-four hours or so. She wasn't in love at all. Phew! For a moment there...

"That's it *what?*" Deb demanded to know.

"Yes, Josie. What's up?" Lisa chimed in.

Josie looked at her roommates and decided it was high time, not for a total confession, but for some bringing them up to date with the new her. She was totally fed up with their thinking she was some kind of born-again virgin.

"I'm going to call Callum, not wait for him to call me. He gave me his cell phone number. And you're right, Deb. I'm not only going to ask him out, I'll be putting out as well."

Deb looked flabbergasted while Lisa just grinned and told her to go for it.

"I aim to," Josie said, and stood up. "In fact, I'm going to go and call him right now. If you'll excuse me, I'll be using the pay phone. My cell phone bill is already high enough to climb over."

Not true, actually. With business being so bad, it would probably be the lowest bill this quarter since she'd started up PPP. Privacy was the name of the game here, not penury.

Josie's inner edginess increased as she hurried over to the phone in the far corner, her feelings bordering on panic that Callum might not answer, or give her the answer she wanted, if he did. This kind of addiction was even worse than cigarettes. It would take some time to recover after Callum had left next week. Going cold turkey would have a new meaning. She couldn't hope to find someone else to take his place in a hurry. Lovers like him didn't exactly grow on trees. But she wasn't going to think about that now. She'd cross that bridge when she came to it.

Callum answered straightaway, sounding grumpy till he realized who it was. Then he sounded even grumpier.

"You don't seem pleased to hear from me," she

said, her stomach in knots of fear that he was going to refuse to see her tonight.

"You're not crying off tomorrow night as well, are you?" he asked belligerently.

"Heavens, no! No, I'm really looking forward to being your call girl for the night."

"Not as much as I am, I'll bet," he muttered, then sighed. "Sorry. I'm a bit strung out tonight."

"Me, too," she said shakily. "Is it...er...too late to change my mind?"

"About what?" he asked warily.

"About tonight."

There was a deafening silence down the line.

"Callum?"

"Sorry, you surprised me. Yes, I guess you can change your mind. I haven't taken the uniform back yet...."

"What uniform was that? You never did tell me."

He laughed. "That's for me to know and you to find out. When you get home. When will that be?"

"Would ten o'clock be too late?"

"Yes. But it'll do. See you then." And he hung up.

When Josie returned to her very eager friends, she had no trouble looked happy and excited.

"He had his phone turned on," Deb guessed. "And he said yes."

"Yes."

"Fantastic!" Lisa crowed. "Where and when?"

"Tomorrow night. We're going somewhere for drinks and dancing."

Deb beamed. "That's great, Josie. Then back to his place or yours?"

"His, possibly." She wasn't sure of his plan yet. But she did have some of her own.

Deb laughed. "You just don't want to do the dirty deed in your mother's house. That's it, isn't it?"

"Not at all." Hardly, Josie thought with dry amusement. They'd already been screwing their brains out there all week. "I just thought I'd like to see his place." And she did.

"Which is where?" Lisa asked.

"He has a terraced house in Glebe."

Deb looked impressed. "That's getting to be a very trendy area nowadays. He must be rich."

"I think he bought the place quite a few years ago. I don't think he's all that wealthy. I'd say just comfortable. He's not old enough to be really wealthy." And he spent far too much on cars and clothes.

"Comfortable is nice," Lisa commented, nodding. "Nothing worse than really rich guys. They think they can treat you like garbage."

"Yeah," Deb agreed. "Rich guys are total bastards. There again, poor guys can be total bastards too. *And* guys who are comfortable. So you watch yourself, Josie. Don't go getting your hopes up over this guy. Just have some fun and games."

"Right," Josie said, and wondered what kind of uniform it was Callum had hired.

It was a policeman's uniform, complete with a sergeant's cap. He was waiting for her on the porch when she got home and for a split second she didn't recognize him. She thought he was a real sergeant from the local station, come to tell her something about the robbery.

"Callum!" she exclaimed when she got close enough to recognize him. But once she did, her eyes filled with the hunger which had been building in her since she'd called. "My, but a uniform does become a man, especially a man with a body like yours. It's very sexy."

"I'm pleased to hear that, ma'am. Now would you please unlock the front door and step inside?" he said, his voice and manner one of abrupt authority.

She couldn't help it. She laughed, then unlocked the door.

"This is not a laughing matter, ma'am." His face remained deadly serious as he followed her into the hallway, closing the door behind them. "I've been reliably informed that you are in possession of drugs and you are going to have to be searched."

"Really?" She had to bite her bottom lip to stop herself from laughing some more.

"Yes, really. Now turn around, put your hands high up on that door and spread 'em."

"*Spread 'em?*"

"Your legs, ma'am."

"My legs..." Suddenly she didn't feel like laughing. His eyes met hers and she swallowed.

"If you don't do what I ask, ma'am, I'm going to have to handcuff you." And he indicated a lethal-looking pair hanging from the side of his belt.

Josie just stared at them, her mouth going bone dry. The thought of being totally helpless before him excited her unbearably, but Kay had warned her not to do anything like that. But Josie was seriously tempted.

"I don't have any drugs on me but search all you

like.'' Dropping her handbag on the floor, she turned and placed her hands high on the door as ordered, moving her legs apart.

''Wider,'' he snapped.

Josie sucked in but did as he wanted. This fantasy was surprising her with how exciting it was. Whoever had thought up these erotic games knew what they were doing.

He patted her quite roughly down over her clothes, paying special attention to her breasts, going over and over them till her nipples felt like rocks inside her bra. Then his attention dropped to her legs, of which a lot was on display. She was wearing a short black skirt and a three-quarter-sleeved pink cardigan top. Sheer-to-the-waist skin-toned panty hose covered her legs. Her shoes were black, and reasonably high-heeled. Josie liked wearing high heels despite being tall. They showed off her slender ankles.

Callum's hands ran up and down each leg a few times, his touch softer and slower than before. He also always stopped just short of where he would have found out how wet she was. Even so, his light caressing of her stockinged skin brought her out in savage goose bumps.

When his hands abandoned her altogether, it was a struggle not to beg him to touch her some more, and much more intimately.

''Can't find any drugs on you,'' he said brusquely. ''But a professional courier like yourself often keeps them well hidden. I'm going to have to strip search you, ma'am. Now, do you want to be cooperative and remove your clothes yourself? Or will I have to do it for you?''

She whirled around and stared, wide-eyed, at him. He couldn't mean... He wasn't going to...

His blue eyes gleamed with devilish intent.

"I'm waiting, ma'am."

"I told you," she said, her heart hammering against her ribs. "I...I don't have any drugs on me. Or inside me."

"I'll have to check that out for myself, ma'am."

"But I don't want you to...to..."

His eyes softened as he reached out and gently touched her face. "Trust me."

"I am. I just..."

"I won't do anything you're not comfortable with, Josie."

Her fear melted away with his sincerely spoken reassurance.

"I know," she said. "I'm being silly."

"Oh, no. Not silly. Never silly."

"I do trust you, Callum."

He smiled. "I'm glad. So what's it to be, ma'am?" he asked gruffly, getting back into character.

"I...I think I'll undress myself."

"Then hop to it. I haven't got all night to waste."

Her hands were trembling as she reached for the zip on her skirt.

19

A LARGE HAND CLAPPED down on Callum's shoulder from behind. "Callum McCloud! I thought that was you."

The voice rang a vague bell, but Callum couldn't put a name to it till he spun around from the bar and came face to face with the one guy Callum didn't care if he ever saw again in his entire life.

Gavin Kittering had been Callum's nemesis during his college days, much like Amber had been Josie's at school. The eldest son of a wealthy North Shore family, Gavin had been one driven dude. His father had expected him to follow in his highly successful engineering steps and Gavin was determined not to disappoint him, despite not having a head for math, or physics. Who knew how he got into the engineering degree course at Sydney University in the first place. Friends in high places, probably.

Anyway, he befriended Callum during his first term, then tried to bribe him to do his assignments for him. When Callum refused, Gavin had found some other poor sucker. But from then on, Gavin had Callum in his sights.

During the entire four years of their course, Gavin

tried to undermine or outdo Callum every chance he got, though not openly in front of others. Sneakily, behind Callum's back. On the surface he pretended to be still buddy-buddy with him, but Callum wasn't fooled.

"Gavin," Callum replied with a wry smile. "Long time, no see. You're looking good." And he was. Gavin had the kind of blond-haired, blue-eyed, lantern-jawed looks which would have won him the leading role in one of those teen movies. He'd have been the football jock who always had the prettiest girl on his arm.

"So are you, man," Gavin replied. "Great tan. Who's that hot-looking babe you're with?" he added, nodding over to where Josie was waiting for Callum at a table.

"She's just a friend."

"Friend? I recognize a working girl when I see one, mate. She got a number? I might give her a call sometime. She's got great boobs. And fabulous hair."

Callum's hands balled into fists but he kept them staunchly by his side. Don't let the bastard bother you, he told himself. He'll sue you if you hit him.

"Josie's not on the game. She just likes to dress extra sexy." Dressing extra sexy had been part of tonight's fantasy. Callum had spent considerable time scouring the shops for the right outfit and had found just the clothes in a boutique in Oxford Street. Tight black leather hipster pants and a matching midriff top which buttoned up at the front, its low squared neckline just covering Josie's nipples.

"Josie, eh? What's her last name?"

"Forget it, Gavin," Callum snapped, his patience wearing very thin very quickly. "She's not for sale."

"Everyone's for sale," Gavin said smugly, "if the price is right. I just underestimated your price. Look, if you won't tell me her name, then I'll ask her myself."

Gavin was off, forcing a path through the crowded smoke-filled bar at considerable speed. Callum launched himself in hot pursuit.

"Hey! Where do you think you're goin', bud," the bartender called after him. "Your drinks are here. If you don't pick 'em up and pay, pronto, I'll call for the bouncer and you'll be leaving all right. On your butt."

"Charming," Callum muttered as he returned to throw some bills on the bar and snatch up the two glasses. Beer for him. Dry white wine for Josie. "Keep the change. Call it a goodbye present," he added sarcastically. "You won't be seeing me again."

"No skin off my nose. We have more customers than we want in here every single night of the week."

Callum could see that. Though it was puzzling. The décor was nothing to write home about and the service stank. This time, the Internet had come up with a real lemon. He'd wanted a sophisticated singles bar to bring Josie to for some fantasy foreplay, not some cramped dive filled with smoke and lecherous guys leering at every female who came in.

If Josie hadn't been with him, she'd have been driven mad warding off passes. As it was, the looks she'd been given were downright X-rated. And Gavin Kittering was busy making straight for her while *he* was being hassled and bustled. Half of his beer was ending up on the floor and he'd made little headway through the throng as he tried not to spill Josie's wine as well.

Callum scowled his displeasure at the situation. He'd made a mistake bringing her here in more ways than one. He'd thought he'd get a kick out of other men looking at her and desiring her and yes, thinking she was his for the night, all bought and paid for. And he'd thought Josie would enjoy the role-playing as well. What woman didn't harbor a secret fantasy to be a high-priced call girl for one night?

The trouble was, while she looked incredible, the outfit he'd poured her naked body into less than an hour earlier *was* over the top.

Devastatingly sexy, though. No wonder Gavin's tongue was hanging out.

Damn, but he just wanted to get hold of that guy and shove his head into a sink, and turn on the taps. Because that's where his filthy tongue belonged.

Josie, Callum could see from across the room, was looking agitated. Whatever Gavin was saying to her wasn't going down too well.

JOSIE HAD BEEN SITTING THERE, wishing she was anywhere else when this big fair-haired guy suddenly dragged up a chair, spun it round and plonked himself down next to her.

"Hi there, gorgeous," he said. "And before you tell

me to get lost, I'm an old friend of Callum's. The name's Gavin. Gavin Kittering. We did engineering together at Sydney University.''

Josie relaxed slightly at this news, though she was still secretly wishing Callum had taken her to a classier place. And she heartily wished she wasn't dressed in this appalling outfit. Talk about trampy. And so tight it was positively indecent.

Sexy, though. She had to admit that since putting it on, she'd been hotly aware of every inch of her body.

''Is that so?'' she said politely, not really liking this guy despite his being very good-looking.

She glanced over his shoulder to see Callum being knocked into by a group of loud guys swarming toward the bar. He was looking very frustrated.

''And you are?'' the blond giant inquired.

''Josie,'' she said.

''Josie what?''

She didn't answer. She wasn't going to give out her last name to any guy who frequented *this* place, even if he was an old buddy of Callum's.

''You're a cool one,'' he complimented, his eyes all over her. She almost shuddered with revulsion. Callum, come back. Quick!

''I like that. Yeah. I like it a lot. Look, I was asking Callum about you at the bar just now and he said you were just a friend, not a girlfriend or anything.''

Josie knew it was foolish for her to mind what Callum said about her, but she did. ''Did he say that, did he?'' she said coldly.

Gavin laughed. ''I see old Callum's still up to his

old tricks. He had a nickname at university, you know. Love 'em and leave 'em McCloud. If a girl lasted a week with him they were lucky. Of course, he probably didn't have the energy for a steady girlfriend, since he was sleeping with our math professor as well.''

Josie gasped. ''Callum was having an affair with a professor?''

''Yes, our math professor was quite a woman. Not bad looking for an older broad, either. She had this… er…penchant…for young guys. It was common knowledge around the faculty that she chose a new student each semester, but Callum lasted longer. I think he actually thought she was in love with him. He acted like an idiot for a while after she finally dumped him. But not for long. After that, he was worse then ever where the chicky babes were concerned. Went through them like a wheat chaffer. Though for pity's sake don't tell Callum I told you all this. He's got the filthiest temper. Broke a buddy's nose once, just for saying something he didn't like. Speaking of his temper, I don't think Callum's too thrilled with my talking to you. So *I'll* love you and leave you for now. Here's my card. Call me sometime if you decide to stop slumming it and go where the quality action is. Bye, honey. I'm outta here before lover boy gets back and blows a fuse.''

Josie was sitting there fingering Gavin's business card and feeling very mixed up in her head when Callum made it back to the table.

"You didn't give that creep *your* card, did you?" he snapped as he sat down.

"No, I didn't," she snapped back as she dumped Gavin's card in the ashtray. "Not that it's any of your business if I did, since I'm only a friend of yours, according to you."

Callum froze with the drinks hovering just above the table, his eyes furious. "That bastard. He couldn't wait to put the knife in, could he?" The drinks finally hit the table with an angry thump, spilling some more of the beer. Callum's sitting down and dragging his chair up close was just as noisy.

"So what else did he tell you?" he demanded to know, blue eyes blazing. "Whatever it was, take it with a grain of salt. Gavin Kittering always hated my guts. If you want an inkling of our relationship at university then think of Amber and yourself and you'd be halfway there."

Gavin's voluntary outpouring of uncomplimentary information about Callum suddenly made some sense to Josie. But was it all lies? Somehow, she didn't think so.

"He said your nickname at university was love 'em and leave 'em McCloud and implied you went through more females than Casanova."

"What?" Callum jumped up, his head jerking round as he searched the crowd. "Where is he? Where is that bastard?"

"Sit down, Callum," she said curtly. "He's gone and it doesn't really matter what he said now."

"It does. He had no right to go dragging up ancient

history and making me look bad, just so he can get into your pants.''

''You can't deny that the nickname is still relevant,'' she pointed out tartly. ''You as much as admitted to such behavior yourself.''

''No. I admitted to having several relationships with women over the past few years, but each one was based on mutual respect and needs. I never used or abused those women. That's not the same as indiscriminately engaging in casual sex with one partner after another.''

''And that's what you did at university?''

''Yes,'' he confessed curtly. ''Yes, that's what I did and I'm not proud of it. But I'm nothing like I was back then. Nothing at all. Hell, Josie, when I first went to university, I was just a kid, a kid with far too much responsibility. I had no money for going out. I had no fun in my life at all. But the girls liked me and some of them threw themselves at me. I took what they offered, which was free and easy. I became addicted to the immediate release of casual sex, and I didn't much care if the girls I was with got hurt along the way. I figured they knew the score since they were the ones making the running.''

''Was that why you got caught up with your math professor? I gather she made the running as well.'' And obviously didn't cost him any money, Josie realized. All she wanted from Callum was sex, too.

Callum shook his head. ''What *didn't* Gavin tell you?'' His sigh sounded weary, but resigned. ''Look, I guess that's part of it. My mum had just died and

Rowena asked me to her rooms for what I thought was going to be tea and sympathy.'' His laugh was rueful. ''And that's exactly what I got. A re-run of *Tea and Sympathy*, but a very X-rated version.''

''She seduced you.''

He laughed. ''In no time flat. Frankly, I'd never encountered anything like that. She was an incredibly confident woman, very experienced, with a dominating and demanding personality. I thought I was in love with her and she with me.''

Josie remembered what Gavin had said. ''Maybe she was,'' she said, her feelings a strange mixture of sympathy and jealousy. ''Gavin said you lasted longer than most.''

Callum's eyes lifted from where they'd dropped to the table. ''What?''

''Apparently, her student lovers only usually lasted one semester. Maybe she dumped you because she was getting in too deep, and it frightened her.'' Just like me, came the sudden and *very* frightening thought.

''Maybe,'' he said slowly. ''But that's ancient history too, Josie. I don't care anymore about Rowena or what she felt back then or what I felt. What I care about right here and now is not having you believe I'm some sort of callous womanizing jerk because I'm not. I care about you, Josie. I really do.''

Did he? If you believed the warmth in his eyes then yes, he did. But only as long as she kept on meeting his sexual needs. She was just another in that long line of sexual partners. Callum's dressing them up with words like respect and caring didn't change the fact that the bottom line was sex. And plenty of it.

Which up till a second ago had been fine by her. She'd been with him all the way.

Josie stared at Callum and wondered what he'd do if she called it quits, right now. Would he care? Or would he just shrug and walk away?

She didn't dare try it. His walking away would kill her. As much as she worried that she might be falling in love with him, her lust for him was still too strong for her to walk away. She wanted him. Now. Tonight. And every other night till his physically leaving would bring an end to it all.

Only then would she worry about whether she'd given him her heart as well as her body. Till then, she aimed to focus right back on fulfilling all ten fantasies while she had the chance.

But on her terms in future. There'd be no more swanning around in public looking like some super slut on the prowl.

"I don't think you're a jerk," she told him truthfully. "I know a jerk when I see one and Gavin Kittering's one big jerk."

Callum smiled. "I knew you had good taste."

"Yes I do, which is why I don't like this place, or what I'm wearing. Please don't misunderstand me, Callum, I appreciate the trouble you went to, finding and buying this outfit. I honestly thought I'd enjoy wearing it for you. *And* in public. But I don't. I especially don't like the way the men in here have been looking at me. Or the things Gavin thought about me.

What we've been doing together, Callum…it's been incredible. I've loved it. And I want to continue till you leave. But strictly in private from now on. Fantasies are meant to be private, don't you think?''

"Yes," he agreed. "Strangely enough, I've been feeling exactly the same thing. I thought I'd like parading you around in public in that outfit, but I can't stand the way the guys in here have been looking at you. It's been eating away at me.''

Josie felt some satisfaction at hearing this. Callum might not love her but he did feel some possessiveness toward her, which was rather nice. "That's another thing Gavin said about you. That you had a filthy temper and that you broke a friend's nose once over nothing much at all.''

"Huh! He's lucky he got off so lightly. He said I was all brawn and no brains, and I had no right to be taking up a spot at university that someone with real class could be filling. So I showed him that he was right.''

Josie shook her head at Callum, but her eyes were smiling. She actually admired him for standing up for himself with his fists, even if it wasn't politically correct these days. There was something very attractive about a guy whom you knew would not hesitate to fight to protect both his honor, and yours.

Callum was just such a man. A compulsive womanizer he might be, but he did have some good qualities.

"I'm really sorry, Josie," he said softly, and reached over the table to take her hands in his. "I didn't mean for tonight to work out this way. I guess you're not cut out to be a call girl.''

''Oh, I don't know,'' she replied, whipping her hands out of his before she went to mush. She had to get their relationship right back on track, and quick. ''I've drawn up this list....'' And she dived into her shiny black evening purse, producing a smallish sheet of paper. ''There aren't ten things this time. I could only think of five. I've written my charges beside them. Have a look and tell me what you think.''

Callum's eyes dropped to read the list.

1. Strip tease—$50
2. An all-over massage—$50
3. Hand relief—$50
4. Oral relief—$75
5. Straight sex in whatever position the client prefers—$100

Callum's heart twisted as he read what was really a very simple and straightforward list. Obviously, Josie didn't know the endless number of seriously kinky things call girls did for their clients.

She really was an innocent. Which was what would make her doing any or all of those five things for him so very special.

''Your prices are a bit steep,'' he teased.

''I know. But I'm good.''

''How good?''

''You'll find out after you've shown me the color of your money.''

''I didn't bring much cash with me.''

''Damn. A clever call girl only ever takes cash. And

in advance. But you're right. I'm just not cut out to be a call girl. So I'll take an IOU.''

She grinned at him and he grimaced back. Hell, but he already had a hard-on. Thank goodness this place was crowded or just the act of leaving could be embarrassing. He'd make sure she walked out first so he could hide himself by pressing up behind her. Close. *Very* close.

''Do you have a pen?'' he asked.

''Right here.'' And she dived back into her purse. ''This call girl might be a pushover but she's got a pen. And six condoms,'' she added on a husky whisper. ''One's even strawberry flavored. My favorite fruit.''

''Fantastic.'' He scrawled an IOU at the bottom of the list and handed it over.

''A thousand dollars? For that, you'll have to have more than one of each. A *lot* more!''

''True. But there are ten positions on that other list of yours back home. And there are a couple we haven't tried yet. There's one even *I* haven't tried before.'' Woman on top, back to the man, in front of a full-length mirror.

Who knew why he hadn't tried it since it sounded perfect for both partners, but he just hadn't.

She stared at him, her eyes becoming glazed. It seemed that position had stuck in her mind too.

''Don't worry, I'm good for the money,'' he said.

''I'm not worried about the money,'' she told him in a breathy little voice. ''You can have unlimited credit.''

"In that case I'd like to start with number four on your price list. If you recall, we're parked in a very dark corner of the carpark so no worries about privacy. You can use the strawberry-flavored condom if you like," he added ruefully when her eyes flared wide.

"What? Oh, yes. Yes. Er...um...whatever you say," she replied, obviously struggling to recover from her shock. But she managed, finally finding composure with a saucy little smile. "The client is always right."

His smile carried both admiration for her boldness and genuine enjoyment at the moment. "You know, I could get used to games like this."

Me, too, Josie thought breathlessly as he pulled her to her feet and started propelling her toward the exit, and the carpark.

20

KAY WAS WORRIED. *Very* worried. Josie had been off with the fairies all week. Totally distracted. Kay was pretty sure she knew the reason. Her boss had fallen in love with that Callum guy. The signs were all there.

But what could she do about it? Nothing much.

Still, she'd really like to meet this Mr. McCloud in person. See what he was all about.

Kay glanced up at the kitchen wall clock as she started filling the kettle to make tea. It was just after nine. Katie had finally gone to sleep—overtired after a long day at preschool. Colin was ensconced in his study, doing his Friday night paperwork. Kay felt tired herself after a hard week, as well as somewhat tense over tomorrow's auction. If it didn't go well, then she'd probably be looking for another job.

Josie had claimed today she was tired too, and said she definitely wasn't going out tonight. Callum was supposedly coming over for a quiet evening of watching videos.

Kay suspected they wouldn't be watching videos for too long, but they probably wouldn't have gotten down to the nitty-gritty at this early hour. Now what excuse could she find to call Josie and wangle to meet this Casanova in the flesh?

The light of inspiration went on in Kay's brain. Yes, of course. The auction tomorrow. That was it. Perfect!

Dashing into the family room, Kay picked up her phone, settled in the very comfy armchair next to it and punched in Josie's home number.

On the seventh ring, Kay was about to hang up and try Josie's cell phone when a man answered, sounding slightly out of breath. "Yes?"

"Callum?" Kay tried. After all, who else could it be?

"Yes. Who's this?"

Mmmm. He had a very nice voice. Very masculine but not too deep. "It's Kay." Kay knew Josie had mentioned her to him so he should know who she was.

"Oh, hi there, Kay. I suppose you'll want to speak to Josie. She's watching this video and she's totally wrapped up in it, but I know she'll want to talk to you. Still, best I take the phone to her, rather than get her to get up and come out here. I'm in the kitchen."

"I'll bet it's a romance," Kay said ruefully. "That girl's hooked on romances."

"I wouldn't call it a romance. It's more of an action movie."

"That's surprising. Josie's not usually keen on action flicks. I like them myself but she always complains that they have no women in them."

"Well there's definitely a woman in this one. She's gorgeous too. And very sexy. I suppose it could be classified as an erotic thriller."

Now Kay understood the attraction. "What's it called?" Maybe she and Colin could watch it together sometime.

"*Bound To Be Bad.*"

"I've never heard of that one."

"It's only a very small-budget movie."

"That explains it, then. I only ever remember the blockbuster kind."

"I'm walking into the room where Josie is right now. Josie, it's Kay."

"Wait! There's something I want to ask *you* first."

"She wants to talk to me first," Kay heard him tell Josie. "You can keep on watching your movie for a while. Shoot, Kay."

"Josie's told you about the auction tomorrow, hasn't she?"

"The apartment at Manly, you mean? Sure has. She says it's looking fabulous, thanks to you."

"That's nice of her to say so. But I've been thinking that maybe the living room furniture needs rearranging. I've become a fan of Feng Shui just recently, and I was checking up on the placement of the furniture and I shouldn't have put the couch directly opposite the sliding glass doors. I'd like to change the furniture in that room before the apartment is open for inspection tomorrow. The trouble is that couch is as heavy as lead. I know Josie plans to arrive at the apartment reasonably early. But I'm just a weak little thing myself and Josie can't lift that couch by herself. Do you think you could come with her and help move those few things for me?"

"Love to. I've heard so much about that apartment I'm curious to see it. I might even stay for the auction. Would you mind?"

"Heavens, no. No, that would be great. We could

have lunch together afterward and celebrate. At least, I hope we'll be celebrating.''

"I'm sure you will."

"I'm not quite as confident as Josie. Rain's predicted for tomorrow. Kiss of death for some auctions, though at least this one's inside. Thanks for that, Callum. Perhaps you'd better put the girl herself on now. I think I need to remind her personally about the flowers and fruit. She's been a bit distracted this week. I wonder why,'' she added with a wry laugh.

He laughed back, an amused but warm laugh which curled around Kay's heart and made her hope that Josie might have found herself a winner this time. Lots of men said they didn't want to settle down till they met the right girl. And Josie was one very special girl. If Callum didn't see that, then he was just plain stupid. Or just plain bad.

Yet he didn't sound stupid. Or bad. He sounded nice.

JOSIE COULD NOT BELIEVE that this was happening to her. Callum had been expertly doing the number one thing women liked men to do to them in bed when the phone had rung. She'd begged him not to answer it but it had amused him to abandon her right on the edge, the sadistic devil. He'd been gone for what felt like ages, though it was probably only a minute or two, and then he'd come wandering casually back into the room, chatting away to Kay like they were old friends, even promising to go to the auction with her tomorrow.

Panic immediately replaced arousal. Josie didn't

want him to go to the auction. She didn't want him to
intrude into her real life. She wanted to keep him
safely in her fantasy world, the one confined to night,
never day. It was the only way she would survive this.

Last night, as Callum had propelled her from that
awful bar, she'd determinedly boxed up her entire fling
with him in her mind as total fantasy from beginning
to end. She'd pretended that hadn't really been her last
night, going down on Callum in the car, or doing a
very provocative strip tease for him after they arrived
home, or wallowing in the position of the night for
over an hour. It certainly wasn't her bound naked to
this bed now. This was someone else. Someone wild
and wicked and yes, wanton.

Callum's covering the mouthpiece of the phone
with his hands and coming to sit beside her on the bed
snapped her right back to her earlier crippling state of
sexual tension. If he touched her now...

"How much have you told Kay?" Callum asked
softly.

"Nothing about this," she choked back, her eyes
glancing down at her spread-eagled legs then up to
where her arms were stretched tight, her wrists cuffed
together then chained to the wrought-iron bedhead.
"Do you honestly think I would?" And she shuddered.

The look he gave her was odd, as though she'd hurt
him somehow. But maybe she was imagining it, because suddenly, he was smiling and it was the sexiest
smile. She knew that smile. It meant he'd thought of
something even more wicked.

When he tucked the phone firmly under her chin

then ruthlessly resumed his earlier activity, she groaned a tortured sound.

"That you, Josie?" Kay asked. "Or the movie."

Both, she thought, and looked dazedly up at where Callum had set up a video camera on a tripod at the foot of the bed. It had a small television screen attached which showed what was being filmed. Josie was finding it an incredible turn-on, watching herself and Callum together.

"The movie," she managed to answer, hoping she didn't sound like a woman struggling not to come.

"Must be good. I won't keep you long. Just wanted to remind you about the flowers and the fruit."

"The what?" She couldn't concentrate, couldn't think about anything but watching the way her eyes were growing wider and wider. She wanted to wriggle but if she did, the phone might drop away so she kept stiffly still. Perversely, that only seemed to make things worse.

"The flowers and the fruit," Kay said wearily. "You said you'd buy some fresh in the morning."

Sheer force of will—and fear of total shame stopped Josie from moaning and groaning. "Yes, yes," she said, desperation creeping into her voice. "I haven't forgotten."

"I can hear that you want to get back to your movie. Must be a good one. Hey…I thought you said all the televisions and video players in the house had been stolen. Surely the insurance company couldn't have replaced them that quickly."

"No, no. Callum brought his own over."

"Why didn't you just go to his place?"

Josie could hardly tell Kay that Callum's bed didn't have wrought-iron bed-ends with places to attach chains to. ''I thought I'd better stay home since I have to be up early in the morning. Look, I'll see you tomorrow.''

''No later than ten now. Don't you dare sleep in.''

''I won't,'' Josie agreed through gritted teeth.

''Bye. Have fun.''

Kay hung up just in time.

21

CALLUM WAS IMPRESSED with the apartment. On today's market, it was well worth the five hundred thousand reserve, and he told both the girls so.

He had nothing but praise for the way they'd decorated and presented it, especially the color scheme. He would never have thought to put blues and greens together, but they complemented each other perfectly. He'd never been overly fond of white kitchens and bathrooms, either, thinking them cold and clinical, but once the deep terra-cotta bowls of colorful fruit had been added to the breakfast bar and vibrant yellow towels hung in the bathroom, both rooms looked bright and inviting.

The irises Josie had bought this morning looked fabulous in the deep blue pottery vase sitting on the glass coffee table. Just the right touch for that room, as was the large blue-framed mirror hanging on the wall adjacent to the balcony, and which cleverly reflected the ocean view.

If only the sun would shine…

As it turned out, Kay had been happy with where she'd originally put the couch. Frankly, there just wasn't anywhere else to put it, and like she said, the sliding glass doors were more windows than doors. So the couch stayed right where it was.

All the furniture, rugs and paintings were from Josie's father's rental division, but the finishing touches had been bought, or borrowed. The bowls and vases dotted around were originals from Mrs. Williams's studio. The rest of the purchases—such as the tea towels, towels and various other knickknacks—had come out of the company's petty cash. Josie explained that while she wouldn't be out of pocket too much if the auction failed—her father wouldn't make her pay for the furniture—if there was no sale, then the survival of PPP was at risk.

Unfortunately, the one big dampener on the day so far was the rain. It was literally pouring down outside, which was a real shame given that the apartment's main asset was the view. On seeing Josie's downcast face Callum decided then and there that if the darned thing looking like being passed in, he'd bid for it himself. He'd been going to buy another investment property, anyway.

Admittedly, this place was more up-market than he usually bought, but what the heck? He couldn't have his woman being depressed.

His woman…

Now Callum was in danger of becoming depressed. Because what was the point of thinking about Josie as his woman? She didn't want to be his woman. All he was to her was her fantasy lover, good for one thing and one thing only.

He'd come to this conclusion this morning when she'd been less than pleased at having him accompany her here, and in having him meet Kay. Clearly, the lady boss of PPP preferred him consigned—and confined—to her bed.

But *she* was the one who'd been confined last night, he reminded himself. It had given him great satisfaction to have her at his mercy, to torment her over and over, to have her moan and beg, to witness the total surrender of her will, as well as her body, into his hands.

And he'd taken full advantage of that surrender. A fitting revenge, perhaps, for her not caring about him as he cared about her.

He hadn't been aware of his vengeful motive at the time, although perhaps subconsciously he'd already known his feelings for her had grown deeper, even as hers were becoming more shallow.

It was all very ironic, given he was the one who'd first offered himself as her fantasy lover. *He* was the one who'd worried that *she* might want more from him that he could give. He was the one who'd been concerned that she might be too vulnerable for a strictly sexual affair.

What a joke *that* was!

Yes, it was ironic all right. But perhaps all for the best. He *couldn't* give her what she really wanted, which was marriage and children. He could only give himself. And that wasn't enough. Better he did love her and leave her, and then she could find herself some other guy who'd be willing to go the whole hog. At least now she wouldn't feel she'd missed out in the sexual department. She'd have done it all, once they'd completed the ten fantasies.

Well…not quite all. As much as fantasies nine and ten were quite raunchy, involving sex toys and some seriously kinky lingerie, they weren't beyond the pale.

And tonight's fantasy, number eight, was the sweetest and most romantic of all. It was called THE TOTAL INDULGENCE FANTASY, with the man doing absolutely everything for the woman's pleasure. Callum had spent all yesterday getting everything ready.

The setting was to be his house this time, because he had a roomy corner spa in his en suite bathroom, a necessity for the scenario he had in mind. The scented bubble bath was sitting on the vanity, waiting to be used and a myriad of candles were dotted around the bathroom, waiting to be lit. Brand-new white satin sheets were on his bed, and he'd already put some romantic music into his portable CD player. A very expense love lotion was at the ready, erotically packaged in a glass bottle shaped like a nude woman. *He'd* be the one giving the massage this time, and he aimed to take his time.

But first, of course, came the meal, served on a candlelit table, with expensive champagne which would put Josie in the right romantic mood for some slow sensual lovemaking. Callum had enjoyed acting out all the fantasies so far but he was in the mood for something different tonight, something softer and gentler and yes, something more loving.

His heart turned over at that thought. Damn, but he'd been the one burnt this time, hadn't he? Now he knew how previous girlfriends had felt when he'd

moved on. Love had a real problem with moving on.
Love wanted more. And more. And more.

"I wish it would stop raining," Kay said as she slid
back the glass doors and stepped out to where he was
standing on the balcony.

"So do I," Callum agreed, glancing up at the
gloomy skies. "The real estate agent's arrived, I see,"
he added with a glance over his shoulder.

"Yes, open house starts in five minutes. I hope we
have a good turnout. And I sure hope this sale goes
through. If it flops, it'll throw Josie for a loop. She
pretends to be a confident person, but she has her insecure side."

"Don't worry. I won't let the sale flop," Callum
said, and Kay threw him a surprised look.

"You mean you're going to bid?"

"I'll buy the place if I have to."

Kay stared at him and he knew he'd revealed far
too much.

"Don't tell her," he said sharply.

"Tell her what?"

"You know what. You are a very intuitive woman.
I'm leaving on Tuesday for the States and that's all
there is to it. I am what I am, Kay, and I'm not what
Josie wants. It's better she doesn't know that I've
fallen for her."

"How can she not know anyway? I know, and
we've only just met."

Callum smiled a dry smile. "Josie's wearing blinkers at the moment."

"Blinkers?"

"Red-colored glasses. They're even worse than

rose-tinted specs when it comes to women. The brand name is Lust."

"If you think all she feels for you is lust, then you're wrong."

Callum's heart jumped. "Has she said she feels more?"

"No…"

Callum sighed. "Then you're the one wearing rose-tinted spectacles, Kay. You don't know Josie as well as you think you do. Trust me on this."

"What are you two talking about out here?" Josie called out through the still open glass doors.

"I was just inviting you and Callum to a barbecue at my place tomorrow. He said he'd love to come."

Callum almost laughed. Both at Kay's optimism, and the look on Josie's face—it was not the look of a woman in love.

"He did?" Josie said, and lifted cool eyebrows at Callum.

Callum shrugged. "I never knock back a home-cooked meal." Again, he was being a bit spiteful, knowing Josie didn't want to have to go anywhere where she had to treat him like a normal boyfriend.

"Look!" Kay exclaimed. "The sun's coming out."

So it was, the clouds melting away. As did the frostiness emanating from Josie, her eyes suddenly sparkling again.

Callum wished she would look at him that way. With sparkling eyes, not chilly ones or even smoldering ones. Neither extreme pleased him.

His mood sank farther into the depths.

Despite the emerging sunshine, the two hours of

open inspection was not a great success, with only about twenty people coming through, not many for an apartment in a prime position overlooking a North Shore beach. Only half that number stayed for the actual auction. How many were genuine prospective buyers was debatable, but probably only three or four.

As it turned out there were only two, with one dropping out at the four-eighty mark. The remaining bidder looked sharp to Callum. He was in his mid-thirties, a slick dresser with the kind of dark-eyed, dark-haired, slightly foreign looks which a lot of women went for. He'd eyed Josie up and down when he'd first arrived, which hadn't exactly endeared him to Callum, so when the bidding stalled at four-ninety, the other guy dropping out, Callum stepped into the breach.

"Half a million," he called out, and Josie's head snapped round to stare at him. Fortunately, she was standing right away from him, Kay having deliberately drawn her off into a far corner, knowing he was going to bid.

"What's he doing?" Josie hissed into Kay's ear.

"Getting us a good price," Kay whispered back. "So hush up."

The other bidder, whom their agent had told Josie earlier was a top drawer real estate agent representing an overseas client, didn't bat an eyelid at this new bidder. Which was just as well. Hopefully, his client was a multi-millionaire with money to burn.

"Five-ten," he said quietly with a slight nod to the auctioneer, and Josie breathed a huge sigh of relief. Callum was off the hook and at least they had a sale.

They wouldn't make much on the deal but it was better than nothing.

"Five-twenty," Callum came back after a few seconds' hesitation.

"Five-twenty-five," the agent retaliated, still with a poker face.

"Five-thirty," Callum countered immediately, and for the first time, the other bidder showed a slight irritation.

"Why doesn't Callum just shut up?" Josie groaned under her breath, her heart racing on pure adrenaline.

Kay didn't answer.

"Five-forty," the agent bid again, probably hoping that by raising the bid ten thousand, he'd frighten Callum off and seal the deal. But no, Callum shot back with five-fifty and Josie thought she was going to have a coronary.

"Five-sixty," the dark-haired gentleman bid, and Josie held her breath.

Don't bid, Callum. Please don't bid.

She watched his mouth open, then slowly close. With a scowl, he crossed his arms at that juncture and stayed blessedly silent while the auctioneer went through his last-minute cliff-hanging spiel before the gavel came down and it was a done deal. Only then did Josie dare to breathe again.

"Kay! Do you realize we've just made over eleven thousand dollars! PPP lives to fight another day."

"That's great. Now look, we can't go near Callum for a while," Kay warned her in low tones, "or it'll look like a setup."

"Yes. Yes. You're right. But, brother, I'm going to

have a word with him later on. What did he think he was doing?''

"I think he was doing you a favor," Kay said dryly. "So anything you have to say to him should start with thanks."

"But what if he'd got left with it?"

"He didn't. Let's go congratulate the winning bidder," Kay suggested before she blurted out to Josie that Callum was madly in love with her. Not a good move at this juncture. She had to be cleverer than that.

"He isn't the actual buyer," Josie said. "He was representing someone else. He's a real estate agent."

"All the better. He might be able to throw some more business our way. After all, he's seen some of our work at close hand and clearly approved of it."

"You're right. Why didn't I think of that?"

"Perhaps because you can't think of anything else but Callum McCloud lately," Kay said. "You're in love with him, aren't you?"

"Aren't you?" she repeated when Josie didn't answer.

"There's no point in discussing it, Kay. Callum's leaving on Tuesday and that will be that. And I can't complain. I knew the score. I'll survive."

Yes, Kay realized. She would. And so would Callum. But they'd never be the same again. Josie would become harder and tougher, then marry some other man, using her head and not her heart. And Callum would regret letting Josie get away till his dying days. He might think at this moment that he didn't want to settle down or embrace any more responsibility, but life on his own would one day become very lonely, and empty, and boring. At thirty, it might be exciting to be footloose and fancy free. But what about at forty, and fifty and sixty?

Kay had one chance to show these two that they were meant for each other, for life, not just for a fling. And that one chance would come tomorrow, at the barbecue! Colin would help, Kay knew. He was a fan of family life. Katie would be a persuasive force, too, though she wouldn't realize it. She just had to be her enchanting if cheeky self and Callum would get a different perspective on parenthood.

"Come on," Kay said breezily. "Let's go see if we can get ourselves some more business."

22

"IF YOU DON'T WANT to do this anymore, Josie," Callum said somewhat testily, "please just say so."

Callum's question surprised Josie, though not his tone. He'd been in a bad mood ever since the auction, though she wasn't sure why. In hindsight, he'd been acting contrarily all day. First, he'd accepted Kay's invitation to a barbecue tomorrow, *knowing* Josie didn't want to pretend anything about their relationship. And then he'd shocked her by bidding for the apartment. That had really floored her.

After everyone connected with the auction had left, and she'd been able to question him about his unexpected bidding, Callum had offhandedly explained that he'd been in the market for an investment property, anyway. He'd surprised her with the news that he was already the owner of several apartments around Sydney, purchasing one each time he'd saved enough for a deposit. Most of the rent from the tenants covered the mortgage. A sound business strategy, if you could afford it, which he obviously could.

"I don't usually buy on the North Shore," he'd elaborated, "but it seemed an excellent opportunity to kill two birds with one stone. Help you get a decent price and me a new rental property. Still, when the bidding went over my valuation estimate, I was happy to leave the other guy to it.''

But he wasn't happy, Josie could see. He hadn't been happy all afternoon, not during their celebratory lunch with Kay down at the Manly Hotel, or later, when they'd driven back to her parents' house, primarily to return her mother's pottery to the studio. He'd been impatient over her taking her time there to also shower and change. And obviously irritated when she'd then rung Lisa and Deb to tell them about the success of the auction.

Of course, getting her roommates off the phone was never an easy exercise. They'd wanted to know the ins and outs of everything. They'd inevitably asked about Callum too and she'd admitted she was going on a date with him tonight. She'd been dismissive on Lisa's speculation that perhaps Callum might want to date Josie on future visits to Sydney, stating quite truthfully that she had no intention of being at Callum's beck and call for years to come. She wanted a man with his feet on the ground, thank you very much. And with a yen for fatherhood. Someone who lived and worked in Sydney as well. Sydney was her home. She never wanted to live anywhere else.

When she'd finally hung up half an hour later, Callum had grumbled over the amount of time she'd kept him waiting.

His complaining had irritated her. A lot. Deb and Lisa were long-term friends who'd been there for her during some tough times. She'd promised to ring them after the auction, and a promise was a promise. Callum was just a passing item in her life. Her friends would be her friends, long after he'd flown off into the wide blue yonder.

So maybe she should be saying, *Yes, Callum. You're quite right. I don't want to do this with you anymore.*

Josie had known since her last night's outrageous behavior—so much for her resolve never to be tied up!—that the wise thing would be to stop seeing him. And the sooner the better. But she was a woman in love, not some unfeeling robot. There were more compelling forces at play here than cold hard logic or common sense.

As Callum drove through the early evening light toward to his home in Glebe, Josie's body was already anticipating the evening ahead. The yearning had started. And the need. Impossible to stop at this juncture, especially when tonight promised so much. She'd been thinking about it all day while desperately trying not to. That was the one of the reasons she hadn't wanted Callum at the auction. Because being business-like with him around was too darned difficult. She only had to look at him and her mind projected ahead to tonight's fantasy.

It was so unlike all the others. It was romantic, for starters. Sensual, but caring. Highly intimate, but still loving. Tonight, she could pretend that he wasn't just her fantasy lover but her dream man, as madly in love with her as she was with him. The other fantasies had been exciting, but tonight was going to be super special. Memories would be made tonight, Josie knowing that of all the nights she spent with Callum, tonight would be the one she'd remember the longest.

"You seemed pretty taken with that Drake guy," he said at length. "I thought you might be looking for a change in lover."

The penny dropped and Josie almost laughed. Callum was jealous. Not jealous jealous. Possessive jealous. The male ego at its worst double standards. Callum wasn't offering her anything permanent, but Lord help her if she looked sideways at another man.

Josie was tempted to tell him as much, but she didn't want to argue. She wanted tonight to be a night to remember, and not for all the wrong reasons.

"I was not attracted to Drake Carson," she said calmly.

"Then why did you give him your card?"

Josie rolled her eyes but kept her temper.

"The man's a real estate agent, not a guy on the make. After the auction, he congratulated me on the way PPP had presented the apartment. He said he might have a few clients for us. Kay was with me, if you recall. We exchanged cards for business reasons."

"Doesn't mean he won't ask you out," Callum grumbled.

"True. And I'll say no, since Mr. Carson registered quite high on my jerk meter. But business is business and I can't go looking a gift horse in the mouth. Look, I shouldn't be putting up with this from you, Callum. You aren't a real boyfriend, you know. But you sure are sounding like one."

Callum winced.

There it was, his opportunity to say but I *want* to be your real boyfriend. I love you, damn it. Come with me overseas. Live with me. Travel with me. Be my real girlfriend. Not for a few weeks, or a few months or even a few years. Maybe for forever.

But such a proposal was dead in the water before it could be made. He'd overheard what she told that roommate of hers. She'd stated quite clearly that she'd never live anywhere but in Sydney. On top of that, she wanted a man with a yen for fatherhood, certainly not a man for whom the thought of having children made him want to run a mile. Callum was not what *she* wanted. He never would be.

So he stayed silent, smothering his personal pain with the thought that if he loved her, he'd let her go.

"I didn't say that to hurt you, Callum," Josie went on, perhaps sensing some of his feelings. "But there's no use pretending. We agreed to a fling and a fling's all I want with you. It's all you wanted too, if you recall, so why the attitude all of a sudden?"

"I guess I'm just being a typically possessive male. Sorry."

"No need to apologize. Just lighten up. We only have three days left together. Let's make them fun."

JOSIE STIRRED the second Callum climbed out of the bed.

"Where are you going?" she mumbled in a soft slurry voice which reflected her soft slurry state. When he didn't answer straightaway, one eye opened to see a naked Callum padding his way across the bedroom.

"To the bathroom," he threw back over his shoulder. "Go back to sleep."

She closed her eye again but the damage had been

done. Her brain had clicked into gear at the morning light, her memory of the night before filling her mind.

Fantasy number eight had been everything Josie had imagined it would be. And more. She'd been entranced from the first moment Callum had led her inside his elegantly furnished terraced home and shown her how much trouble he'd gone to. The candlelit dinner had been perfect, and highly romantic. As had the spa bath and massage afterward. By the time Callum had started on the serious lovemaking, Josie's whole body had gone to mush. Her mind, too. For the first time, it had felt like Callum really loved her, and wasn't just using her for sex, and vice versa.

Too bad it had just been a fantasy.

The toilet flushed and both Josie's eyes flicked open. Callum emerged from the bathroom but he didn't return to the bed. He started pulling on a gray track suit.

"Now where are you going?" she asked, levering herself up onto one elbow, the white satin sheet falling down to her waist.

He walked back into the room, his eyes skimming over the still hard and incredibly sensitive tips of her breasts. He'd kissed them endlessly last night. And licked them, and sucked them. Josie doubted they'd ever go back to normal.

"I jog most mornings," he told her as he sat down on the side of the bed and pulled on some battered trainers which must have been lying under the bed.

"You didn't go jogging in the mornings after you stayed over at my place."

"Yeah, well I've been slack, haven't I? It's time to

get myself back into gear. I have to be back to work this week. See you in an hour,'' he said brusquely. ''Go back to sleep.''

Josie couldn't go back to sleep, of course. Callum's ''morning after'' brusqueness had confirmed what had started between them yesterday. With the end of their fling on the horizon, Callum was already gearing up to moving on. By the end of next week, he'd probably be looking around for his next woman.

Dismay at this thought—and at his curt attitude this morning—created a secondary reaction. While Josie had found last night quite wonderful, the prospect of enacting out the last two fantasies with Callum now brought instant revulsion.

She couldn't bear the idea of his using all sorts of coldly clinical implements on her. Or his wanting her to strut around for him in nipple revealing bras and crotchless panties, or whatever other kinky lingerie he'd bought from that online adult sex shop he'd found. Josie conceded that all those things could be fun, if your partner loved you. But not when he didn't. Not when you were only one in a long line of no-strings sex partners.

That was just not right. It was tacky, and demeaning.

No, enough was enough. She would have to call a halt to this. And today.

Josie's heart twisted at the thought. Leaving Peter had taken courage, but this was much harder.

''Oh, Callum,'' she sobbed, and turning her head into the pillow, she wept. But not for too long. If she cried for too long her eyes would be all red and puffy and Callum might twig to her loving him.

Her tears had subsided to the odd sniffle when the sound of the front door opening caught her attention. Had Callum come back early?

Hearing a male whistling as he virtually ran up the stairs sent her sitting bolt upright in the bed. Callum never whistled. She was in the act of clutching a sheet up over her naked breasts when a handsome but alien head popped inside the open bedroom doorway.

"Ooops," Clay said on sighting an obviously naked girl in his brother's bed. Wow, he thought, having glimpsed perfect breasts and perky pink nipples before taking in big dark eyes and long tousled black hair. Callum had certainly taken his advice. Here was *some* woman. "Guess I should have knocked. But the door was opened. Callum in the john, is he, honey?"

"He's out jogging. And my name is not honey," she added tartly. "It's Josie. I presume you must be Clay."

"Josie," he repeated, frowning. "God, not the...."

"One and the same," she interrupted crisply.

Clay frowned, then grinned. "That sneaky devil. He conned me about why he didn't come home last Saturday night, didn't he?"

"You could say that," she said in bristly tones. "But no big deal. It's nothing serious, so don't buy your best man's suit just yet."

Clay laughed. Ms. Josie Williams had an acid sense of humor. He wondered if Callum liked that, and if he also knew how stuck she was on him. There was no other reason for her to be this sarcastic. The free and easy kind never bothered. They just enjoyed the sex and as much of your credit card as they could get away with.

"So did you get the part or not?" Josie asked and Clay's eyebrows shot up again.

"He told you about that, did he?"

"He had to come up with some reason for why it wasn't you doing the escorting that night."

"Aah. I see. Well, look, honey…er, I mean Josie. I've just got in after one hell of a long flight and a week in the States, and I'm desperate for some tea and toast. So why don't you pop on some clothes and join me in the kitchen and I'll give you the lowdown on me and Hollywood. Callum been gone long?"

"About half an hour."

"Right, well he won't be back for another half hour. Callum runs his life to the clock. Most of the time, that is," he added, looking Josie up and down again. Maybe things were a changing with his big brother. Maybe Callum had finally joined the human race.

"I can't get up till you leave," she pointed out dryly when Clay just stood there, staring at her.

Clay shot her a cheeky smile. "Gee. What a shame."

"I take my tea with milk," she countered in droll tones. "With one sugar."

Clay laughed. Brother, was Callum in trouble with this one. "Tea with milk and one sugar coming up," he replied, and headed downstairs, smiling his satisfaction with the world all round.

CALLUM RAN like he was in training for a marathon, punishing his body in the hope that his mind would shut down through weariness and give him a break.

But the tactic didn't work. His thoughts revved up, if anything.

He couldn't keep doing this, he decided by the time he made it back to his street. He had to end it *now,* this morning, as soon as he got back. He didn't think she'd mind all that much. She didn't want him taking her to that barbecue at Kay's today, anyway. If she was desperate to experience those last two fantasies, then she could explore them with someone else. Not him. He'd give her the damned stuff he'd bought for them, if she wanted.

Hell no! No, he wouldn't be doing that, he wasn't that generous, or self-sacrificing. Just the thought of her having normal sex with another guy killed him. The thought of her prancing around in front of that slimy sleazebag Carson in that X-rated black lace corset he'd bought—the one with the suspenders and little else—made Callum seethe with the darkest jealousy.

The sight of his front gate being open brought him up with another jolt. He never left his gate open. But maybe he had. He wasn't himself this morning. When the front door wasn't locked, however, Callum knew something was up. Worried, he dashed inside, expecting the worst.

The sight of luggage dumped near the door brought relief. Clay was back. But without giving Callum any notice, naturally. No phone call. Nothing. That boy!

But alongside Callum's exasperation lay disappointment for his brother. Clearly, things hadn't worked out for him in Hollywood.

The sounds of voices coming from the kitchen stopped Callum from going upstairs. Clearly, Clay had already made his presence known to Josie. Callum headed along the downstairs hallway and pushed open the bar-style louvered doors which led into the kitchen.

The sight of the woman he loved perched up on one of the pine stools, laughing at something his brother had just said and looking incredibly sexy in one of his shirts, made Callum's teeth clamp down hard in his jaw. He was in a bad way.

"Callum!" Clay burst out. "Guess what? I didn't get the part."

Clay's cheeriness at this news seemed weird.

"But not to worry," he went on with a big grin. "They gave me a better part, in a movie they'll be shooting at Fox Studios in Sydney, starting next month. I already have a three-movie contract, a hundred-thousand-dollar advance and a brand-new Hollywood agent to attend to matters over there. Harry's been promoted to my personal manager and PR man. I've made it, bro. I'm going to be a movie star!"

The unexpected and enormous pride and joy which consumed Callum at this announcement brought two highly uncharacteristic responses. First, he raced over and gave his brother a big bear hug of congratulations, clapping him on the back and telling him how wonderful he was. Second, as he glanced over his brother's shoulder and caught Josie's eye, his own eyes suddenly threatened tears.

He quickly swung Clay around and blinked the tears

away but the shock of his almost weeping in front of them sent him looking for escape. Excusing himself as soon as possible, he dashed upstairs for a shower, his mind going round and round as he tried to come to terms with what was happening to him here.

In the end, Callum didn't tell Josie he wanted to call it quits. And he still took her to the barbecue. But he was one very bewildered man. Everything he'd always thought about himself was in danger of falling apart. All his life decisions suddenly seemed silly. He was at a crossroad, and he didn't know which way to turn.

23

"IT'S NOT WORKING," Kay muttered as she tossed the salad.

Colin glanced up from where he'd been overseeing the sizzling steaks. "What's not working, love?"

"*That!*" And she indicated where Josie and Katie were playing together in the back yard and Callum was sitting in a nearby deck chair, sipping a light beer and watching them both with a dark frown on his face.

"I thought when he saw us together, and Katie, and Josie *with* Katie—you know how good she is with her—that he'd change his mind about family life and having kids."

"Mmmm. Not a good idea, Kay, meddling and matchmaking. Your mother used to try that with you, remember? All to no avail till you were good and ready. Besides, you're wasting your time. Callum told me he's leaving for the States this week. Tuesday, I think."

"Yes, I already know that. I was hoping he'd change his mind, stay in Sydney and marry Josie."

"Goodness, that's a leap of faith, isn't it? They've only known each other a little over a week."

"There are weeks and there are weeks. I think their

week has been rather intense. Josie is crazy about him.''

"Well if it helps, I think he does care about her."

"I *know* he cares about her. He told me so. But he refuses to tell Josie he's fallen for her and made me promise not to. He says he doesn't want marriage and kids, but she does and it's best if he leaves her to it. I'm not sure if he's being noble or just plain stupid."

"Just plain stupid, in my view. Marriage is great."

Kay looked over at Colin and smiled. "You're just saying that because I gave you a massage last night."

He grinned. "It wasn't the massage but the extras which sold me. I'd almost forgotten how good you are, woman, at being bad."

"I know. But back to Josie and Callum. I...."

"Look, I wouldn't worry too much about Josie and Callum, if I were you," Colin cut in. "They're both smart people. If they truly love each other, they'll work things out."

"I hope so...."

"The steaks are ready!" Colin called out to his visitors. "Come and get it!"

JOSIE HAD HAD two viable excuses for putting off telling Callum she wanted to call it quits so far that day. First, there'd been Clay's unexpected return. Difficult to drop her bombshell when the two brothers had been catching up on such good news together. Then she hadn't want to disappoint Kay and not show up for the barbecue.

But both excuses had gone now.

Callum was driving her home and no doubt expected to stay the night. She hadn't asked, but Josie suspected the assortment of sex toys and kinky lingerie he'd already bought for the final two fantasies were stashed somewhere in the car, ready to be produced in a flash in all their corrupting glory.

Josie shuddered at the thought, but at least such thinking gave her the courage to speak up.

"Callum," she began, trying to sound matter-of-fact and firm.

"Yes?"

"I've been thinking...."

"Have you? So have I. All day. And I..."

"Let me say what I have to say first, please," she broke in sharply, not wanting to hear what he'd been thinking about. Because she knew exactly what he thought about during each and every day. The coming night's sex. That was all he ever thought about with her. Sex.

"Oh. All right. Shoot."

Just say it, she instructed herself firmly. Don't waffle. But it was just so hard!

"You were right yesterday," she said tautly. "I don't want to continue with our affair, or fling or whatever you want to call it. I've had enough."

"You've had enough," he repeated, the car slowing appreciably. Finally, he pulled over to the side of the road, turned off the engine and faced her.

"Enough what? Enough sex? Or enough of me?"

"What difference does it make?"

"It makes a lot of difference to me."

"Then let's just say I've had enough of the type of sex we've been having. I still like you a lot, Callum, but I think it's best we don't see each other anymore. You're leaving on Tuesday, anyway. It's been great. You've been great. But enough is enough.''

"Right. I see....'' And he fell into a darkly brooding silence.

Josie's stomach swirled as the silence grew. And grew. "Could you please just take me home now?'' she finally blurted out when it seemed he was going to sit there all evening.

"Fine,'' he snapped, and started the car up again.

Neither of them spoke during the rest of the drive home. By the time Callum pulled up outside her house, Josie was desperate to get inside where she could safely cry her eyes out. She had never felt this desolate, or this depressed. And she'd been pretty desolate and depressed during her marriage to Peter, *and* after.

"Don't I get a kiss goodbye?'' Callum growled when she reached for the passenger door handle.

Oh God...

She turned to face him, terrified that her feelings would be there for him to see, in her face. Better she did kiss him. That way, she could at least close her eyes.

If only he hadn't taken her chin in his hands with such a gentle touch. If only his lips hadn't been so soft, and so sweet.

Her sob was telling. His head lifted and his eyes locked onto hers.

"You've been lying to me, haven't you? You don't really want me to leave. You love me. Say it, Josie. Say it!''

"I...I love you," she choked out, her eyes filling with tears.

"Then why were you calling it quits?"

"Because there's no point, is there? You're leaving on Tuesday."

"Yes. Yes, I am. But I'll come straight back if you want me to, Josie. You only have to ask."

Confusion mixed with elation. "But you said..."

"I wasn't in love with you when I said all that crap. Everything's changed now."

Josie's world tipped sideward before righting again. "You're in love with me?"

"I adore you. And I can't live without you. I *won't* live without you. I might not make much of a husband and a father but I'm willing to give it a go. I'm even willing to live in Sydney. I'll quit my overseas job and get something local."

"But you'll hate that. You love doing what you do."

"Not as much as I love you."

"Oh. Oh, that's so sweet," she cried, her heart overflowing with emotion. "But I can't let you do it."

"*What?* You're knocking me *back?*"

Callum could not believe it! All day he'd been in a turmoil, sorting out his feelings, coming to terms with them, making compromises and plans for their future together and now here she was, the girl who was the catalyst for all these mammoth changes, telling him not to bother.

"I'll go overseas with you," she counter-offered, stunning him. "I'll give Kay control of PPP. She'll make a success of it, I know she will. You don't have to marry me or have children. We can live together and travel together. I know you don't really want to be a husband and father.''

''But you're wrong. I *do* want to, with you. I realized that today. In fact I realized quite a lot of things today. My first revelation came when Clay told me of his success in Hollywood and I felt a happiness and a high which none of my own successes had ever brought me. It was what a father must feel when his child does something great. There's just nothing like it, Josie. There's no selfishness in it, just pure joy. It staggered me for a while. I couldn't take it in. But seeing Kay with her husband—and seeing you playing with their delightful little girl—showed me that marrying and having a family wasn't all about sacrificing and suffering. There was great happiness to be found in commitment and caring. Great...satisfaction.

''When my mother was dying, she told me that she'd never regretted having me and Clay; that we'd given her a lot of joy. I didn't believe her at the time. I thought she was just saying it to make us feel better. But I don't think that now. I know she meant it. She loved us, in much the same way I love you. Unconditionally. So I'm asking you, my darling girl, please marry me.''

The eyes which searched his face were still slightly unsure. ''You really mean that, Callum? It's what you really want?''

''It's what I really want. I'm done with running away from life, Josie. Of course, I wouldn't mind your coming with me and traveling with me for a while.

Maybe a year or two. There's so many exciting places overseas I'd like to show you.''

"Then that's what we'll do. I wish I could come with you on Tuesday but I can't. I don't have a passport for starters, and I really do have to stay here and mind the house till my parents get back. I'll also have to sort things out with Kay about PPP. I could be ready to go in about three weeks, though. Would you be able to fly back here and get me?''

"I'll be back by next week at the latest. No way am I going to let you go cold on me.''

"As if I would...'' As if she *could!* She burnt for him all the time.

"I'm going to ask your father for your hand in marriage properly too, so that he knows I'm serious about you. And we'll be married within six months. No waiting too long for that. Then, when we eventually come back here to Sydney to settle down, we'll try for a child straightaway.''

"Child, Callum? Only one?''

"No. Not if you want more. But I would dearly love to have a little girl like that adorable Katie. Make a change from raising a boy. Though I do realize you can't order up something like that.''

"Oh, I don't know. Kay and Colin wanted a girl and Kay bought this book which guaranteed a girl. And she got a girl. Of course, you might not be happy with doing some of the things Colin had to do.''

Callum was almost too afraid to ask. "What did he have to do?''

"Abstain from sex on certain days. Follow a special diet and wear boxer shorts. None of those tight jocks.''

"Doesn't sound too tough a deal. I could do all that."

"Even abstaining from sex for quite a few days each cycle?"

"Sure. No big deal. I'll have you know I didn't have sex once during the three months before I met you."

Josie was amazed. "I thought you were a sex addict!"

"Who me? Nah. Not me. But my appetite has sure picked up since meeting you. Which reminds me. What are we going to do about all that kinky gear I've got in my trunk? Send it back?"

"Seems a shame."

"That's what I was thinking. Do you have to go to work tomorrow?" he asked, and Josie's eyes widened.

"No," she asked warily. "Why? What did you have in mind?"

"I'd like to take you engagement ring shopping."

Josie's heart flipped right over. Engagement ring shopping.

"I'll take a day's sick-leave," she said swiftly.

He laughed. "Will the boss mind?"

"Nah. Kay's cool. Lord, just wait till I tell her she's the new boss of PPP. She's going to flip. Over everything." And so were Deb and Lisa. Josie couldn't wait to call and tell them.

But she *would* wait. Till tomorrow. She had other plans for tonight.

There were only two fantasies to go. Perhaps they could be incorporated into one, leave tomorrow night free for other celebrations. Her friends were sure to want to organize something before Callum left on Tuesday, even if he was returning next weekend.

Her eyes slid sideways and met Callum's.

"Are you thinking what I'm thinking?" she said.

"What are you thinking?" he returned.

"That I'd like to see what you bought for those last two fantasies. Up close and personally."

He grinned. "I'm glad that becoming engaged hasn't changed you."

Josie smiled secretly to herself as she climbed out of the car. Little did he know but becoming a safely engaged woman *had* changed her. It made her feel totally good about being totally bad.

Suddenly, Josie's fantasies had become limitless.

When she joined the man she loved at the trunk of the car and started looking at the wickedly erotic goodies he'd bought, she couldn't hide her delight.

"I'm not sure I like the look of that smile," Callum said warily.

"Aah, but you will, darling," she said, her eyes sparkling saucily at him. "You will."

HARLEQUIN® *Blaze*™

From: Erin Thatcher
To: Samantha Tyler;
Tess Norton
Subject: Men To Do

Ladies, I'm talking about a hot fling with
the type of man no girl in her right mind
would settle down with. You know, a man to
do before we say "I do." What do you think?
Couldn't we use an uncomplicated sexfest?
Why let men corner the market on fun when
we girls have the same urges and needs?
I've already picked mine out....

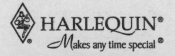

HARLEQUIN®
Makes any time special ®

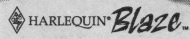

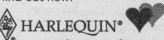